Alwyn Dow is a much travelled and experienced author with three previous publications to his name. He says that his books, including this one, are a mixture of fact and fiction and therefore, works of 'faction', a term coined by Truman Capote. He adds that his underlying themes always include individuals faced with moral dilemmas in the circumstances in which they find themselves. *The Dawn Birds* takes some inspiration from *The Thorn Birds,* but is set in Africa.

I would like to dedicate this book to my neighbours and the staff at St Richard's Hospital, Chichester, as well as, at the War Memorial Hospital in Bognor Regis. I could not have completed this work without their encouragement during and after a long stay in hospital following a fall. Their commitment to me, as to others, was palpable, reinforcing my mum's firm belief (and mine) in the goodness of the human spirit.

Alwyn Dow

THE DAWN BIRDS

AUSTIN MACAULEY PUBLISHERS™

LONDON • CAMBRIDGE • NEW YORK • SHARJAH

A CIP catalogue record for this title is available from the British Library.

ISBN 9781398423862 (Paperback)
ISBN 9781398423879 (ePub e-book)

www.austinmacauley.com

First Published 2022
Austin Macauley Publishers Ltd®
1 Canada Square
Canary Wharf
London
E14 5AA

My mum inspired my faith and my school motto was 'virtue, learning and manners,' dictum's hard to follow but very inspirational. My sources are very wide, but I owe a special thanks to Robert E Goode, whose 1973 book, UDI, confirmed and added to my personal experience.

Table of Contents

Introduction

This is a story in which Love, Faith and Loyalty collide over a series of decades and it is set mainly in East Africa. The tale is told in turn by three friends, namely Elda, Luke and Gordon who meet at the UK Birmingham University. She is a young student and is mesmerised by the powerful personality of 'Father' Luke who is a Jesuit priest with ideas that do not always accord with church dogma. Gordon is a Scot student who is more of a free spirit and Elda is drawn to them both. As the story unfolds and tragedy intervenes, Elda and the Dawn Birds are finally able to share a happy ending on Lake Naivasha.

The Dawn Birds

Part One
Elda's Story

Foreword

A solitary sheep bleats mournfully on a windswept Yorkshire Moor in the year of our Lord 680 AD. It is dawn and there is not a cloud in the sky above. The moor is silent but for the calls of the 'Bonxie' or great skuas along the shore. Then, as if to announce the dawn, flights of gulls suddenly appear and begin to swoop over the nearby Whitby Abbey, firstly in hundreds and then in thousands. St Hylda was dead but the Sea Birds of her soul would never allow her to be forgotten. In those moments, a movement was born to carry on her work for social justice and rights with regard to land ownership.

Chapter One
Elda Whitby

My name is Elda Whitby. I don't know why I am called Elda although Mum had said I was named after an Auntie Hilda, but Dad said that with a name like Whitby, there was also a hint of 'St Hylda' of Whitby Abbey who died in 680 AD but it didn't seem to matter much to me until I met Luke at the University.

My brother's name is Hugo and no one asked him either, but Luke was different. He asked me why but I had a sneaking suspicion that he knew much more than I did anyway. He was a Catholic priest, a Jesuit (so I was told) and seconded to the University to teach and 'to learn', he said. Most of his friends were 'in the Church' and some, such as the Ryan twins Peter and John (I could never tell which was which), were also in Opus Dei. My history tutor, Dr Mary, told me that this was an independent 'church within a church' that allowed them a bit more freedom in their faith, but which held a hard line on doctrinal and other matters, even viewing some moderate pleasures as 'sins' and wearing hair shirts. I wondered if Luke did the same because I had heard that Jesuits had a lot to do with the Spanish Inquisition and I didn't feel too happy about that at all.

It was time for some more learning, so I took myself off to the library to give Luke clear licence to proceed to the next stage in our 'romantic' adventure. I was nervous about what I might find because I knew that priests in holy orders were celibate and that would not do for me. Fortunately, I found out that not all Jesuits are priests, but 'clerks regular'. It's true that they made a vow of 'chastity' but that isn't 'abstinence', is it? I felt better and rather suspected that the church and the university did not wish to dwell on these semantics as long as the 'Work of Our Lord' was being done.

To be truthful, I never did quite know where he stood on matters spiritual, but I knew where I stood about matters pleasurable and physical if he only knew it. Sometimes I thought that he did know how I felt because he looked away when I squirmed on my chair. I could see that he was fighting his urges also and taking refuge behind his cassock and collar. Of course, I was very aware that he knew a lot more than I did about many things, because he was the teacher and I the student at The Catholic Newman College of Education. Furthermore, he was 'Father' Luke to me and all the other students, being one of the 'parish' nominal priests for Birmingham University. So basically he was 'not available' and therefore it was another young charismatic teacher who caught my eye. His name was Gordon Bird and I had to smile at the association of ideas with his name and his speciality in ornithology. He saw me smiling and smiled back as if we were sharing a joke already, signalling that I should join his table at lunch which had nearly finished. I looked away shyly and blushed, but nothing escapes the notice of your friends when you are blushing, and it was just my damn luck to run into Sophie and Susie as I came out into the corridor.

"Aha!" laughed Sophie.

"Aha!" said Susie in echo. (Yes, they were just like two peas in a pod.)

"What's up?" asked Sophie.

"Yes, what are you up to, you naughty girl?" said Susie.

I smiled bravely. "Nothing at all. See you at tea!" Then I ran to my study and flopped on the bed with relief. I stared at my Renoir poster as I drifted off in a daze and there was Luke and there was Gordon, and there was Luke until I could keep my eyes open no longer.

My studies did not allow for much free time but there were weekly discos that 'us girls' frequented until the 'lads' appeared after closing time. I never saw Luke there, but I must say that Gordon was a good 'mover', especially when he wore his kilt on St Andrew's Day.

Some months later, I left the university and went into the outside world, back to live with Mum and Dad, but with a small flat of my own in Barnham/Yapton West Sussex so I forgot about it altogether. However, and most unexpectedly, the question did arise again, but this time on my 'new' home doorstep. I was having a coffee outside Barnham station when a man entered and sat at a table on the opposite side of the room. It had been an early start for me, barely dawn when I got up and hurried to the station for a coffee. It was a dank and dreary morning, but as I peered through the gloom, I could see his image in the window as he looked out at a gaggle of squawking birds on the pavement jostling for food. *No it can't be*, I thought, but just then he turned and, yes, it was, it was Luke, *Father* Luke, and I felt myself getting warm all over.

"Hello, Elda," he said, "may I join you for a coffee?" Just like before, I wanted to run, but no, I didn't want that at all.

"Fancy you remembering me," I said coyly as I cleared a space at my table. "It's so nice to see you. You're a long way from Newman. What are you doing here?" I asked, but what I really wanted to do was to touch him.

I noticed that he was not wearing his customary black priestly costume or his white 'dog collar' of which he had been so proud. He smiled as he watched me watching him. "Well, what do you think?" he said mischievously.

I paused, playing for time. "What do you mean?" I replied.

His fingers drummed on the table and I could sense that he was thinking, "You know what I mean, don't you? Why don't you just come out with it?"

However, he was too polite to say so and, after a moment or two that seemed like ages, he looked at me closely and said, "Yes. I left the priesthood many years ago and now I do a bit of teaching and other things." I don't know why but for some reason and for the very first time, I felt a twinge of anxiety about 'my' Luke. This didn't seem like him at all, in fact, he was the most Jesuitical of the Jesuits that I had met before during my 'instructions' in the Faith when I was much younger. I looked out of the window for reassurance, but the birds had suddenly gone silent. However, his next comment took me entirely by surprise. "So you never became a nun then," he said, "Elda's a rather good name for a Nun, I think, don't you? Mind you, the church doesn't leave much room for style and your hair looks rather cute in a bun, but with a name like Whitby, shouldn't you be following in the footsteps of St Hylda? (Shades of my dad here.) Who knows you might even

21

be a 'St Elda' one day." He laughed and I laughed too but what really took me entirely by surprise was his reference to my hair. He had seen me as a desirable woman for the first time and I almost fainted.

However, there was no time for that as he stood and gave me his card saying that he had to catch a train. "Ring me and let's catch up soon," he said and kissed me on my forehead. Then he was gone, clearing a path through the birds who objected strongly, and I wondered if he would be showered in 'guano' on his way across the road. I watched him go then I repeated, "He loves me, he loves me not," and promised not to shower for a month. Yes, I did think about him a lot that week. I was in love, maybe it had been a puppy love back then at uni but now, I can hardly bear to say it, I was 'like a bitch on heat'. *And now he was free, of the church at least*, I thought. *Now we could be one as God intended.* I smiled at my cheek and said a prayer apologising to God for my impertinence. Luke had reminded me of those days when I had sat enthralled at his every word, but not just his because I soaked up learning like a sponge. I studied Sociology and Psychology as well as History and Religious Studies but also Environmental Studies that used to be a 'Cinderella' subject until dark warnings of climate catastrophe dawned on people. I decided that I needed to know more so I added a class at the local technical college hoping to do my bit one day. Also there was Gordon Bird from my college at Newman so many years ago and now he was specialising in ornithology. We had a coffee but those days of the 'Highland Reel' at the disco were well and truly over.

I had now become a teacher myself in the Five Villages Academy not far from home so there was much to do and to learn in my first year. I was lucky to have secured a geography post while a teacher was on maternity leave, but I also picked up a few classes of history on supply. Then fate took a hand as our school minibus was involved in a fatal crash that killed 4 boys and a teacher; the science and environmental studies teacher. The next day, the head teacher called me in and offered me a fulltime post. He said that it was a very sad day for the school but a trip had already been organised to visit the Wild Fowl Trust in Arundel and he would like me to go with Franklyn, who also doubled in French. Francoise and I got on very well so I accepted with some misgivings as I thought that I was unworthy of being given this chance so soon in my career. However, as I did so I vowed that I would always do my very best to be worthy of their faith in me, and for a while, I wondered if things like this were just 'meant to be' a matter of fate or even God taking charge. On arrival, our little gang of boys and girls chattered away as we led them into the grounds of a large lake with islands here and there and, yes, hundreds of squawking squabbling gulls and terns with a separate pool for the luxuriant flamingos. We could hardly hear ourselves think. And then for some reason, I found myself wondering if it would be like this with Luke. *Like a circle in a spiral, like a wheel within a wheel, never ending or beginning on an ever-spinning wheel.* Would it be such a merry-go-round of ups and downs of Fate, God and Love or would it just be fumbles of lust? I smiled at my own thoughts as I decided that I didn't really care which for the moment but, what's more, I needed to protect my own little flock (and my sandwiches) from the hungry flock of gulls that besieged us at the lakeside there in the shadow of Arundel Castle. I wanted to say a prayer but all I could think of was St Hylda. Perhaps they were 'her' birds sent to give me a message, but what was it?

Chapter Two
Finding My Way

In the last chapter, I alluded to my family from Whitby in Yorkshire and perhaps I should add a little more now. Actually that was my dad's side but Mum was a Sussex girl from Chichester. Then, there was Hugo, my brother, and then there was me. My full name is Elda Teresa Whitby and I was born and raised in Easter-gate, a small hamlet bordering the Sussex Downs twixt Arundel, Chichester and the sea. Neighbouring hamlets were Barnham, Aldingbourne, Wester-gate, Walberton and Yapton, a distinctive region or 'manor' from posterity as in Yorkshire, and now known as the 'Five Villages' with the school to match. As a child, I took it for granted that the two 'Gates' were the opposite ends of a now non-existent town, but I was told that 'Gate' was just another name for 'Manor' which was the usual name for land areas in antiquity. *But wouldn't it be exciting to think of long-lost town beneath ours*, I thought as a nine-year-old growing up fast. Dad was an engineer and had travelled south from Yorkshire in the Jarrow March in 1936 and ended up with Rolls Royce as an apprentice in Chichester. He said that the march might not have been that successful but it had been very worthwhile because that's where he met Mum. She was a Catholic and he a bit of an agnostic but he loved her dearly, so I ended up at St Philip's RC secondary school in Barnham and thence on to the Catholic Newman College at Birmingham University where I met Luke (remember him?). Before all that, there was time for growing up and I even had a boyfriend called Roy, but he was just a boy if you see what I mean. I know that because my friend Hazel and I took Roy and his mate Bill into a barn one day and insisted that they 'show us'. Well, there wasn't much to see I can tell you, but Hazel had an older boyfriend and she whispered in my ear and giggled. The boys ran off and we giggled a lot more.

Dad was very attached to his family in Yorkshire and we made our 'pilgrimage' every other year to the triangle of Malton, Pickering and Helmsley near Whitby where the family still claimed ancient rights to our local 'Manor' as traditional 'Gatekeepers' in that triangle. Our responsibilities were to 'see that the good of the community would not be compromised by the greed of the powerful and that common property rights should be protected'. Our family down here in Sussex carried on the old traditions from Yorkshire and many a meeting was held on the floor in front of a raging fire. You can just picture Uncle Joe and others as they sat in council and smoked pipes while I sat on the floor. I had noticed that they spoke alike, being from Yorkshire, but they also all looked alike and dressed alike in a rather dull grey reminding me of the sea gulls I had seen at Arundel, though rather better behaved. After many amicable greetings and drinks, Uncle Joe would hold his hand up for silence and begin his usual monologue. They had all heard it before but everyone listened politely except me, as I was only nine.

'Tell me,' he would begin. *'If a said thing is illegal then surely it must be the case that any other thing that follows as a result of it, must be illegal for all time.'*

The onlookers would all murmur approval at Joe's simple statement or another similar one, and then a member would speak up to ask for a current report by a member of the keepers committee. There were three keepers present, one from each of the hamlets (now towns) that had comprised the Manor where they had lived in Yorkshire. Now they not only claimed a kind of authority over our local Sussex hamlets but 'across the world' as a kind of responsibility to see to it that the vision of St Hylda's seabirds would not allow 'her soul to be forgotten' and that 'might' would never rule 'right' wherever an injustice prevailed. Such ideals impressed me as visions of Terence Rattigan's *The Winslow Boy* in which the axiom 'Let right be done' was key, had made an impression on everyone at that time. Then a certain amount of legal talk usually took place and on one occasion I think that I started to yawn.

"Head up, my girl," said my dad, "You or Hugo will probably be gatekeeper here soon enough." This upset me and I ran from the room, crying.

I have told you a bit about the university and I suppose that I was a good student mainly because I had two very good teachers, who complemented each other in a way. Father Luke taught me about the 'Faith' as he called it, but for him, it was also about the moral imperatives that could trump Church doctrine on occasions. For example, he was a pacifist, more allied to the Quakers than 'Holy Mother Church' whom he saw as tainted by their ambivalent attitude to land ownership that tended to favour large vested interests of property-holders such as those of the Church. He also felt that the Church had become soft, and more discipline was needed; 'in order to set a "Christ-like example," he said without mentioning his Jesuit background. Once more, I felt uneasy at this rather strict uncompromising tone, reminiscent of my catechism classes with the Canon when I was very young but Luke's words reassured me for the time being when he said the following.

"You might have to take sides or make a choice on matters of Faith or the human heart yourself one day," he had said on one occasion, "The issues are not always clear, so just keep your powder dry, don't rush, give things time, and the answer will come to you."

My other 'guru' was my History lecturer, Dr Mary Donaldson, who was a world authority on Medieval Europe and beyond. In fact, nothing escaped her eagle eye as she flitted from the Wars of the Roses to the Spanish Civil War without taking breath. Perhaps it was she, rather than Luke, who opened my eyes to social injustice over the centuries insisting that we read St Thomas More's *Utopia* as well as the complete works of George Orwell. As I said, she was widely read, but she had a special interest in the social cataclysms that enclosure had brought to the country. She didn't say it although she might have done but it was St Thomas More himself, writing in 1516, who identified the enclosures of his day as being largely 'responsible for social problems' in the land. However, Mary had a wider brief and gnawed away at the many injustices that land 'transfers' took over the centuries. In other words, it was not Tudor period in England alone that was to blame but a whole societal culture built on the precept that 'might is right'. For her, all the people owned all the land and it was not divisible by force or even a legal title brought about by coercion. Thus, even in Roman times, the key to success, and thus more land, lay in military advancement or the legal profession. This is somewhat surprising as the Roman Empire did have a strict legal code although little consideration was given to those who were unable to resist tyranny of one sort or another. The Tudor enclosures just speeded up the process as did the later Acts of Parliament from 1800.

And so I completed my education as somewhat of a radical. I knew what I was for and I knew what I was against but suddenly and, as I mentioned earlier, I met up with Father Luke at the Barnham station coffee shop. Had he really shown 'that kind' of interest in me? Yes, he had and I knew I could not be wrong, and from then on, it all fell into place despite some misgivings.

Chapter Three
Love Birds

Complete surprise it may have been but it had seemed inevitable that Luke and I would become lovers one day even before that fateful meeting at the station, but as our 'date with destiny' came closer, I did have my misgivings. Not because of Luke himself but because of my fears of an intimacy that might not survive his past as a Catholic priest. I was reminded of course by *The Thorn Birds* (1977) story in which Richard Chamberlain (Father Ralph) embarks on a tempestuous but tortuous love affair with Meggie whilst still in holy orders. The story is a sad and wistful expose of the impossibility of any permanent future for them. I was just hoping and yes, praying that this could not happen to us but I don't think that Luke gave it a thought. His conscience was clear he said, and he could not do anything that was against his conscience and what is more, he loved me.

"I love you and only you," he said. "My love for Mother Church is part of that love as you are part of me." I was overwhelmed because I felt the same way and, little known to him, had felt like this for ages. So 'our' day finally arrived and we took a short trip to Selsey Bill which is a long archipelago of about 10 miles that protrudes into the sea near

Chichester. Our destination was a small hotel on the cliff edge looking toward the Isle of Wight and we didn't mind at all that a blustery wind greeted us. I wouldn't say that we ignored it because rather we enjoyed it until it was time to retire. I shall remember that moment for ever as he took my hand and said, "I love you, Elda." In our room we became one as dusk settled over the bay and then again as the sun rose to greet the dawn of a new day.

Once more, we were on our balcony overlooking the sea as seagulls whirled overhead, swooping as if to communicate but maybe just hungry for food. It was a lovely moment and I hoped that nothing would ever spoil it, but somehow I felt guilty, or at least inadequate, after what he had said about setting a 'Christ-like' example so I took his hand and said that I had something very important to tell him about me and my family, but where would I start? No time like the present I thought so when we were seated I began. "You know that my name is Elda Whitby but there's a bit more to it than that. You also probably know about St Hylda and Whitby Abbey in pre-historic times but perhaps you don't know about the hundreds and thousands of seabirds that hovered over her grave in the Abbey for months when she died, leading people to believe that wherever the gulls gathered in such large numbers in the future, they would be carrying a warning with a tacit appeal to every generation to see that 'her soul should not be forgotten' and this is where I come in as a member of one of the families of 'keepers' over many generations. Our tactics are legal but our aims are the same as hers. Her priorities in life had been clear, and her 'soul' meant that 'might' should never be allowed to trump 'right' and this meant that the status quo of common land and common rights should be protected at all costs. With no military force to back her up, she relied on the minutiae of legal texts as to land ownership and other matters and that's what we Whitbys and others do today if we uncover deceptions or cheating in the matter of common land rights. We publicise them and call for reversals or restitutions of original rights, but I can tell you that this is not always popular when we come up against landed interests, property developers and even the Church itself.

"So, let me tell you a bit more about her," I continued, "she was a formidable woman of her day, a Catholic who could compromise and a social reformer as far as was possible then. She also had a royal heritage, being related to the Kings of Northumbria at that time. She founded Whitby Abbey in 657 and that is where she died in 680. Her followers wanted a sign, a sign from God maybe, a sign that would enable others through the centuries to continue her work. Their prayers were answered and they got one, and more than one in fact, hordes of seabirds hovered and swooped over her grave for weeks, giving rise to a movement that had to be secret because of the social and religious intolerances of the day.

"Leaders were termed 'Gatekeepers' and one was my dad so now it will be me here in Eastergate when another vacancy falls. My dad has already been replaced by my brother, Hugo, but there are those who think that he might not be up for the job. He's bright all right but perceived to be on the lookout for the good of Hugo and not that of the community. In fact, he has a small property advice centre that he runs in Chichester and he owns the row of shops opposite, including the newsagents and the chemists. The other chair has been occupied for a long time by another close relative of mine who is a local to Barnham, namely my Uncle Wilfrid.

Unfortunately, he is not in good health and he could be around for years but he has assured me that they will give me time to prepare for what lies ahead. The issues may well be local but I've been warned to expect a great deal of resistance from vested interests as has always been the case. Financiers, landowners like the Church of England and many property developers, and even some 'fair weather' friends will find all sorts of ways to protect and even enhance their interests. So I'll have to be very careful." I smiled as I finished this long speech and he smiled back.

"Don't worry," he said, "I love you and I'll always be here for you if you will have me, my own St Elda." The fire was warm but I wanted his warmth to cover me and to take me.

"Well," I said, "love me, Luke: love me now." And, taking his hand, I led him toward the stairs. No birds this time but plenty of stars in my eyes and his.

It was somewhat of a sharp learning curve to become a Gatekeeper but if my brother Hugo could do it, I was damn sure that I could. What is more, I had Luke in my corner as well as the rather frail Uncle Wilfrid and when I got to spend some time with him, it was he who told me about a case that had been going on for a very long time. He said that it would be good for me take it over in order to gain some experience. "While I'm still around," he had said. I had learnt that he had cancer and wasn't expected to live more than a few months and he knew it. It's funny that when people learn such a truth, they become more sanguine and cheerful and that's what Wilfrid was like. He'd had a few days in bed when he called me over to his house to hand me some files.

"Take the top one," he said, "It's marked A for Anderson, that means Dr Angela Anderson Emeritus Professor in

English at Oxford University. The others are important but that one is crucial as a guide because in some way, she was 'bought off' from pursuing any title deed anomalies. It's not clear who persuaded her although we know that an Agency called TLT or The Land Trust did the paperwork but much of that is unintelligible, in a sort of code, I think. She ended up with a whopping discount and was able to buy a farm somewhere in East Africa, they say. It seemed to be a time when land was easily obtained without too many questions asked." This interested me and I was determined to follow it up if I ever got the chance. Just who were TNT, I wondered and the idea of a code intrigued me even more.

"Keep it somewhere where only you can find it and don't tell a soul that you have it," he continued, "Inside there is a simple map to tell you where a large cabin trunk is hidden and that trunk is another case, that of a Mrs Meredith. Our society has been getting close to reconciling the land documents in her favour and contesting the current fraudulent title, but if 'they' get wind that we are closing in there could be trouble. Some of these people will stop at nothing. By 'they', I mean those whose aim is to ensure that we are not able to upset the protocols of privilege with regard to property from which all wealth emanates in one way or another."

By this time, he was getting out of breath and rather flustered so I gave him a moment before I spoke; it all seemed very clandestine to me so I said, "What about my brother Hugo and Luke?"

He frowned and spluttered, "I said no one and I meant no one. Not even Luke or the Holy Ghost herself," he added with a chuckle, "it's not safe, not safe at all, be careful and while I remember, watch out for Brown and Brown." He paused and seemed to be wondering, so I covered him with a blanket, held his hand and promised that I would do as he asked. He smiled weakly, crossed himself and seemed to murmur 'thank you, St Elda' under his breath and then he slept. There it was again 'St Elda' as if I had been given a very special and important role and I didn't even know what it was. Perhaps I should ask Luke for his opinion. Or perhaps I shouldn't. I just wish that I could be more open with Luke, but to be honest, I didn't really know that much about him apart from his strong principles. I had noted that his name was 'Collins' so I wondered if there might be an Irish, even an Irish Republican connection. I was aware that this might or might not make a difference to 'us' but once again, I was aware that I was getting in over my own head.

Suffice for the moment to look after Wilfrid, over the next few days I dedicated myself to looking after him and he seemed to recover a bit, 'in remission' they said, but suddenly he went downhill rapidly and died on the Sunday after the evening Mass that he had attended. There would be an inquest, they said but I couldn't figure out why. After all, he had not been well recently so it might have been expected that he would die from natural causes. However, within a few days, the preliminary results of the inquest arrived with the information that he could not be cremated, pending the results from a toxicology report. This upset me greatly and I complained but it was no use. I even asked Luke if he might intervene but he said there was nothing he could do. I also wondered what Wilfrid knew about Mrs Meredith and why the situation wasn't safe for me. But another part of me urgently wanted to open the file and find the trunk. *Whatever could be in it,* I wondered.

Chapter Four
Friends or Foes

My interest in the trunk would have to wait for a while because there were more urgent domestic matters to attend to. Uncle Wilfrid had been well known and many wanted to attend his funeral but of course this was delayed pending the results of the inquest. Instead it was decided to hold a 'wake' at Arundel Cathedral without the body. Everyone seemed quite sanguine about the fact that the ashes would not be available on this occasion but many intimated that they might not be able to attend next time. This was understandable as many had travelled from Yorkshire and the group rarely met together in public, so it seemed natural that they would make the most of it and that many photos would be taken by well-wishers. However, I was perturbed to observe what seemed to be a group of voyeurs on the perimeters of our family group. Dressed in black they looked like mourners, but their cameras seemed to follow me around and I began to feel a chill run down my back. I clung to Luke who was beside me and I was reminded of his words 'Be careful' and those of Uncle Wilfrid when he said, 'Watch out'. In addition to his health problems, Wilfrid had experienced poison pen letters as well as threats to his life and even so-called accidents on the high street as a pedestrian crossing the road or even on his bike.

I had been told that an inquest was routine in the case of an unexpected death. Although he had been ill, the doctor was adamant that he was on the road to what he termed a 'medium road to recovery', so checks now had to be done to establish the actual cause of death. Dr Robins had attended to my father a few months before but reasons for Dad's demise were 'crystal clear' he had said at the time, "Heart attack, pure and simple, furred arteries and other signs, over a long period so no need for an inquest". The insurance company had sent their agent along just to check, and they had confirmed the doctor's findings. However, on this occasion, they stated that they would not give an opinion until after the inquest which was to be held the following week. I was worried. *Why was an inquest required at all,* I wondered but soon I got part of my answer when there was a knock at the door. A man and a woman stood there in dark identical trouser suits and I took it for granted that they were from the coroner's office.

"Do come in. I haven't got much to say, I'm afraid, but he was a dear old gentleman. Would you like tea?" I added rather nervously because neither of them had said a word up to that point.

"No, thanks," said the woman, "we haven't come about Wilfrid. We've actually come to see you and support you in your hour of need. We are Jehovah's Witnesses and here is a copy of our *Watch Tower* magazine with many tips about bereavement." She nodded to her colleague and he handed over the small booklet but said nothing. I sensed that she was in charge and she made me feel rather uncomfortable. Mum came home a few moments later and I was making her a cup of tea, when there was another knock on the door.

"I wonder who that is," Mum said, "don't let your tea get cold dear." With that I went to the front door and was very surprised to see the 'Jehovahs' again.

This time he spoke first. "We're sorry to trouble you." he said and then she repeated what he had said, "Yes, we are sorry to trouble you but we have just come to warn you."

She looked serious, and I tried not to laugh as visions of Hell and Damnation crossed my mind but I just said, "Warn me against what? I don't need a warning, thank you," but as I went to close the door, they both pushed in and pressed me against the wall as she hissed, "Just be careful, that's all," and then they were gone.

I felt rather wobbly and fortunately Mum came into the hall on her way to the lounge with the tea. "You look as if you've had a shock," she said, "come and sit down and have a nice cup of tea." I did as she said and began to feel a bit better.

"Did you see who that was?" I asked.

"Yes," she replied, "that was Gerald and Jane Brown, I saw them through the window, they own 'Brown and Brown', that mega property developer and according to my friends, they have their eye on more around here."

"No, Mum," I replied, "they were Jehovah's Witnesses out for soul conversion, not land transaction, I think."

"I should know, dear," she responded, "my friend, Jane, works in their office and she says that they use the JW identity as a good opportunity to gain access to properties in which they are interested."

Now the penny dropped as I recalled that Uncle Wilfrid had told me to 'watch out for the Browns'. "Never mind, Mum," I said, "this is a lovely cup of tea and they've gone now."

She smiled and said, "Don't forget that you have a date with Luke later, you'd better get your skates on." I was pleased to follow her advice as I had been looking forward to my 'date' all day and I hoped that I would not have to mention my 'visitors' as I recalled that Uncle Wilfrid had insisted that I tell no one. Fortunately, I didn't have to worry because, after drinks and dinner at his place, Luke swept me smoothly up in his arms and I can barely (good word) remember the rest as his lips confirmed what my breasts already knew, and how so easily we melted as one-twice!!!

There had been little time for talk and he had a meeting in the morning, so he paused only to kiss me and say, "I love you," for the umpteenth time. I had a quick shower (with regret, as his flavour still covered me from head to toe) and then I picked up the *A for Anderson* file. I opened it very carefully. It seemed to be relatively new, but attached to it was another document marked *Meredith*. I sorted through some papers and yes, there it was; another folder with papers in it, *M for Meredith* or *A for Anderson*. Spoilt for choice, I decided to tackle the *A* file first. It began with Wilfrid's very detailed summary as I set out below.

PROFESSOR ANGELA ANDERSON is 64 and a University lecturer of English and was widowed last year. She sold her house and proceeded to buy a new one on the new-build Barnham 'Symphony Estate' for £350,000. The transaction was handled by Torrance Solicitors on behalf of

Brown and Brown Property Developers who had title to the estate on behalf of CONCEPT, the builders of the said Symphony Estate. However, when her papers came through she noted that the vendor was classified as TLT (The Land Trust), not that of Brown and Brown. She pointed this out but was assured by Torrance that it was a mere technicality and that any changes now would delay the sale and might even cause it to be cancelled. Would she accept a price reduction from £350,000 to £300,000 and allow the contract to take place? She thought it was odd but a discount of £ 50,000 was not to be sneezed at so she agreed. She was anxious to move anyway and being a music teacher, she had already bought a sign for her new home. It was 'Adagio' because she said that she wanted an easy life from now on. She agreed to the discount and soon moved into a house of her dreams with a lovely room for her pupils. I had not heard about all this until it was too late to investigate the unusual aspects of the deeds, but I promised myself that I'd try to be sharper next time starting with my next case, that of a Marion Meredith being determined to research it more clinically. File and archive records of WW. January 2010 AD.

This concluded Wilfrid's notes and I paused for a moment trying to take it all in. I think I must have been in shock because I only managed to stay awake for a few minutes before I sank into a deep sleep awakening in a cold sweat after a most frightening dream.

***

I was Boudicca Queen of the Iceni, heading a large force to confront the Romans at Colchester in order to destroy the temple of the deified Claudius and the Imperial Cult. I was content as we had ravaged all before us and I had Luke and my brother Hugo at my side. The night was long but Luke's arms comforted me in the damp air until morning arrived. We then clasped hands and went to our positions in the half-light. My chariot steeds had started to paw at the ground as I looked around for my lover and my brother. I could not see them until the mist lifted, and then there they were, on either side of the Roman General Comulus and waving defiance. My heart sank as they advanced across a muddy field. My forces dissipated and I collapsed on a bale of hay in a barn with outstretched arms calling out, "Who can I trust? Who can I trust?" until I passed out.

***

When I awoke, I was still in Barnham in Luke's flat and what a relief it was. But what did the dream mean? Was Wilfrid right when he hinted that neither of them could be trusted? I just could not believe it because there's nothing more debilitating than a loss of trust, or a love in doubt, and I felt very weak at the knees. *The best thing to do was to get on with it,* I thought so I opened the *Meredith* package and found a small map marked *Treasure.* I looked at it closely and much to my surprise, the so-called *Treasure* was actually in the loft of MY flat. I haven't mentioned up to now that I had bought a flat in nearby Yapton to rent out when I finished at the uni, both as a bolthole for the future and a bit of an investment. Meanwhile it was much more convenient to live at my parent's home. The thing is that the vendor of the flat at the time was Uncle Wilfrid so we had kept it 'in the family' as it were. However, unknown to me, Wilfrid had continued to use it as a cache for his confidential papers, and the map indicated that they were in the loft. I couldn't wait to get there and pick up the trail of the *Meredith* papers.

I had a small Fiat Panda to run around in but as I walked to collect it from outside the flat, it seemed that the car was leaning to one side with flat tyres, and what's more, I noticed a noxious smell of petrol. I backed off immediately and ran inside to phone the police. They were soon there, together with a fire engine and an ambulance, in case I was in shock. I was shocked all right but more like hopping mad as the officer asked me some questions, starting with a reassurance. "It's probably the kids," he said, "We get quite a bit of that around here but can you think of anyone who might wish to harm you?" I smiled. If he had asked me that a few months ago, I would have been offended. The very idea of it was impossible, but now it was all different. "We understand that the information you gave us was for a 22 Acacia Avenue that we believe is the property of a Mr Luke Collins. I take it that you had been staying there." I confirmed that this was the case but to be honest, I didn't really know who my enemies at this stage might be, so I just gave a simple answer.

"Sorry, no, I can't," I said.

"So did Mr Collins have any enemies that you know about and do you know if he was meeting anyone because we had a report that two men were seen in the early hours of the morning near your car?" he continued. Once more, I was at loss as it dawned on me that I still knew very little about Luke at all, so I just repeated what I had said about me. "OK, we'll get the car checked out and towed away as soon as possible," he said, "Just get in touch with the local station later and we'll have to fill in some paperwork."

I thanked him but I didn't know what to do next. If I took a bus or taxi to my flat in Yapton, Luke would wonder what was going on and at this point I couldn't tell him, so I decided to go back into his flat and wait for him to come home. I walked into the kitchen but I began to feel very tired so I tottered into the lounge and fell asleep straight away on the sofa. I was still asleep when Luke came home two or three hours later.

"Hello, hello, what's this?" he exclaimed. "Haven't you got a home to go to, my sweet St Elda?" I immediately burst into tears and told him everything, well; not quite everything; just the bit about the car.

He seemed very concerned and wanted to sort out a loan car on insurance. I told him that I thought this was a good idea, but for now I would settle for a 'snuggle'.

"Coming right up, madam," he said and swept me up in his arms. I was asleep again before I hit the mattress.

A VW Polo arrived the next morning and, as Luke had business meetings, I was able to continue my trip to my flat in Yapton. However, I had now become very cautious, even suspicious if not paranoid, as well as curious but I decided to go anyway. I must admit that the thought of deceiving Luke, even in the slightest form, made me feel rather ashamed and I was determined to tell him everything against Wilfrid's advice when I saw him later in the day. What harm could it do?

I opened the door and as usual, all the mail spilt over the carpet. "Kettle on," I said, then went upstairs. "Let's find the 'buried' treasure." I laughed at my own joke and was up and down in a trice, laying out my treasure in the lounge while I sipped a cup of tea. There was the *Meredith* file, but the trunk also contained a wealth of documents such as I had never seen. I, therefore, decided to catalogue the contents of the box first to see what information lay within. I had already noticed that the provenance of some were quite ancient, and apparently genuine by virtue of hallmarks and other signatories. This would take some time, I knew, so the case of Mrs Meredith would have to wait for a bit. Actually I need not have been too worried because Wilfrid was a meticulous record-keeper so I'll just list a few of my 'finds' as they came to hand.

In summary, the whole thing was a memorial and a testimonial to St Hylda's vision for a fair society in a very unfair world. However, she had not dwelt on the minutiae of people's lives but on land ownership. It was this that had set the tenor of the times and continued to do so. Given that the Romans had such a legalistic framework, she concluded that many transactions since had been illegal, pure and simple. The policy of St Hylda and her followers was to 'locate the evidence', for without it, no transaction could stand and her followers in the SeaBird Society had to be careful for fear of a legal (or even 'illegal') death if they opposed the 'status quo'. I recalled Uncle Joe's words about the importance of documentation, well, here was a start in the trunk. I couldn't resist opening the first one marked *Romans* with Wilfrid's introduction to be beware of copy documents that are not originals, but even so the first one was a revelation, a sort of Domesday Book, but 800 years early.

First document: ROMANS Hill Forts and settlements
ROMANUS PUBLICUS 284 AD EMPEROR DIOCLETIAN
YORK Honorary Roman capital with London
Growth of Romano British Villas and Manors
Influx of wealth from Gaul
ROMAN CITIZENS AND TITLE TO LAND
1/ Arcadius. Helmsley Gate in perpetuity
2/ Aurelius River Ouse fishing for 10 years
3/ Capitas Licence for baker's shop for 3 years

Gosh, this was just what I was looking for. It was a pity that it was just a copy but I was intrigued just the same. Who 'held' the fishing rights after Aurelius, I wondered; but as this wasn't 1086, I wasn't hopeful of finding an answer although I hoped that Saxon and Norman titles might be more informative with regard to land transfers in due course. However, as the entries just went on and on, I began to realise that I was in over my own head, and it struck me that I needed an ally. It was then that I decided to get in touch with my tutor, Mary Donaldson, who lived not far away in Winchester.

The documents continued:

Second document: SAXONS (St Hylda 614-680AD)
Third document: NORMANS Motte and Bailey farmsteads
Fourth document: MEDIEVAL. Enclosure
Fifth document: TUDOR-ELIZ Parliamentary Enclosure
Sixth document: INDUSTRIAL REV. Dark Satanic Fields
Seventh document: MODERN BRITAIN Urban sprawl

More details are in appendices at the back of the book and needed more scrutiny, but for now, I had to see if I could find a genuine illegal transfer and not a copy.

I, therefore, spent many hours rummaging through these boxes, some yielding more than others so I won't bore you with all of their contents. Suffice to say that I was looking for a needle (or needles) in this boxy haystack and it was this. It would have to be nothing less than hard evidence, supported by irrefutable documentation that a particular land transfer had taken place without <u>due authorisation</u>. It would follow that ensuing land transfers would also be illegal. Such a test case (and it could be the *Meredith* one) could well open the floodgates causing today's monopolists, such as the C of E to rescind so-called titles, negotiate or even engage in claims for compensation. As I write this, I am also aware that should *Meredith* be proven or another such case be found, an odour of corruption and lack of trust would seep into the public domain with potentially serious consequences for them. Lawyers would have to be engaged on a gigantic scale by the many landowners involved, so much so that 'settlements and compensations' would be much more likely in the future and that was our aim after all.

This is all very well, I thought, *but what about me?* I had been told that I was in danger and I rather fancy that my car was a first example of such a threat. So what to do? I still desperately wanted to confide in to Luke, but Uncle Wilfrid had warned me not to trust anyone. Maybe my brother Hugo might help but then again, did he have a foot in both camps? Who was it that said 'Abandon all hope, ye who enter here'? This might as well have been written for me, but then there was a glimmer of hope as I opened a file entitled *Dr Mary Donaldson*. She had been my old tutor at the university so I decided to get in touch with her right away.

You might recall that Mary was my inspirational history lecturer at Newman and what she didn't know about enclosure was not worth knowing. Her file and her latest book *When Waste was Good: A critique of Enclosure* had inspired Wilfrid to keep a copy. I was well aware that she was referring to the halcyon days of yore when wasteland was anything but, being home to countless of thousands in more or less harmonious circumstances before partitions and enclosures began in force. I had been a member of the Newman College Alumni so I knew that she was still active in the Green movement, although retired, so I also wanted to share some of my concerns about today's environmental and economic travesties with her. She lived in Winchester, King Alfred's Capital and as that wasn't too far away, I telephoned for a visit. Once again, my relationship with Luke would be put under strain because he knew her from our college days but telling him might reveal something that Wilfrid had urged me to keep secret but if all seemed well, I would tell him afterwards. *No, this won't do,* I thought, *I'll tell him anyway if only to assure myself that I DID trust him.* So I made my excuses about a sick aunt with a heavy heart (hoping I hadn't used it before) and soon I was settled on Mary's sofa in her apartments in the Abbey grounds.

After I told her about my anxieties, she was very sympathetic. "I'm a mere academic," she said, "but it's people like you who can cause trouble for our 'Lords and Masters' (she spoke disparagingly) so you do have to be careful. If I was you, I'd wait a bit before you share your problems with

Luke. I wonder if you remember his friends at Newman, you know the Ryan twins. Well, I attended a pilgrimage at Walsingham a few months back and Peter Ryan with some others from Opus Dei was there so we chatted about old times as well as current affairs as he shares my love of the Green movement. His brother now works for the UN in New York, but Peter stayed in the UK to promote his views that a 'property owning autocracy' was the best way to achieve a fair society. He felt that the Church and other investment agencies are the best guarantor of a Green future; and I think quite the opposite. He is a research chemist at Chichester Hospital now so his department deals with toxicology reports following a suspicious death, and I'm wondering if he handled your Uncle Wilfrid's case." Mary continued, "I don't think I can help much further, but Peter did tell me that he would be meeting with Luke and Hugo quite soon so perhaps you might ask Luke about that," she paused, "but maybe not at this stage, not at this stage, no, leave it until later. Do be careful, dear St Elda, you know that's what they call you, don't you?"

I smiled and said yes, that it had seemed like a joke but now it was becoming quite a burden that I didn't feel prepared for. I then said farewell and thanked her for her interest and concern but as I drove home, I thought that I smelt petrol so I stopped on a dangerous hard shoulder as trucks whizzed by. I got out and checked the tyres as another vehicle engulfed me in spray. Was I getting paranoid?

So, as I turned into my mum's drive, I decided that there was only one thing to do and that was to involve the police as I felt that they might be the best persons to find out 1/ who had poisoned Uncle Wilfrid and 2/ who had sabotaged my car.

However, I had hardly stopped before Mum came dashing out. "Thank goodness, you're here, dear," she cried, "They've arrested Hugo, and Luke has gone to the station. Please get down there straight away. It must all be a big mistake."

Chapter Five
No Harm Done

On hearing that Hugo had been arrested, I hurried to the police station immediately and met Luke in a corridor while Hugo was being questioned.

"Do you know what this is all about?" I asked, choking back a tear. Luke held me tightly, silently and strongly for quite a few moments before he responded. His grasp had made me feel more relaxed and even secure and I felt that I really loved him at that moment.

"I'm afraid I can't tell you much yet," he said, "they have promised to come and talk to me soon so I'm glad you are here as well." I think that I dozed off for a while because I awoke with a start when Luke gave me a nudge. We seemed to have been waiting all night and now it was 5 am.

"They want us to go in," said Luke, "they must think that we might know something about it but I don't, do you?" I agreed but told him that I suspected it would probably be something to do with the damage to my car.

"Anyway, we'll soon find out," I said, as we were shown into a small interview room and seated opposite two uniformed police officers; a man and a woman. She made the introductions, "I'm Superintendent Wilson," she said, "And this is Constable Allen. We have not arrested your brother yet, Ms Whitby, but he is helping us with our enquiries. Please read his statement and comment when you've done so." With that, she handed over a folder and I read…

My name is Hugo Whitby and I've been detained by the police on suspicion of deception and wasting police time. According to them, I have been involved in falsifying medical records in the case of a recent death and attempting to cover it up. I admit that I am guilty but I stress that there was no harm done and no one got hurt. The fact is that my uncle died from natural causes; but in his final months, he had been subjected to threats on his life unless he dropped his investigations into certain property matters and one of them might actually have come off, had he not died naturally. My partners and I saw an opportunity to discredit those persons who had planned to do him harm so we decided to make it look as if he had actually been murdered and so that a number of so-called vested interests would get the blame. We had motive and opportunity and all we needed was a method to introduce a toxic substance after his death (post-mortem) into his blood to complete our plan. It worked a treat and an inquest on the grounds of a 'suspicious death' was called. There were three of us and we had adopted a simple code of identity when we had had cases similar to this in the past. The 'Dark Arts of Opus Dei', you might call it if you knew of such things, but all in a good cause. We called ourselves Tom, Dick and Harry so it's obvious that I was one of them (say 'Tom'). I could supply toxins from my chemist shop while our medical expert (Dick) worked at the hospital and could administer the

*dose. I'm afraid I can't say much more about Harry but I
suppose that he was really the brains behind the whole affair.*
   Signed HW

The Inspector looked at us coolly to gauge our reaction
before she continued. "There is another small matter you
might like to comment on," she said, "And that concerns the
vandalism to your car outside Mr Collin's address, Ms
Whitby. We had been suspicious about Wilfrid's death and at
one stage, we did think that there had been foul play, so we
maintained a secret surveillance at your home, Ms Whitby,
and at that of Mr Collins as well as number of other locations
and soon enough it paid off. We apprehended two potential
arsonists and now we have them, seated there in the other
interview room, name of Brown, go on, have a look. In the
interview, they blamed each other for 'errors' they had made
by not 'seeing to it' that Wilfrid's Meredith investigation was
halted 'one way or another', and you Ms Whitby had a narrow
squeak as you were next in their firing line. I don't think
they'll notice you with their heads deep in their *Watch Tower*
newsletter but it won't do them much good at all. We'll charge
them later." The Inspector paused and looked at us again,
probably waiting for a response but I had none, and Luke
merely shrugged his shoulders as my world fell apart. He had
not hurt me, but he had deceived me and killed my love, stone
dead. I wanted to cry on Luke's shoulder but I was angry.

   "I asked you about the Inquest at the time and you said
that there was nothing you could do. You lied to me just when
I needed you. Do you call that love?" He had no reply, not
even an apology as he left the room. By the time, I had
recovered my composure it was dawn and he had gone, maybe

forever. Was it my imagination or did I hear the dawn birds squawking, 'We told you so, we told you so,' as I walked to my car with a heavy heart.

I was devastated, so much so that I could hardly think about the ultimate success that we had had after a major headline appeared in the national papers, then on the international news. I was sorry that Wilfrid wasn't here to see it but I think he would have just chuckled and said, "Serves them right, the greedy bastards. Bless you, dear St Hylda and my own St Elda."

These were the headlines the next day.

YESTERDAY AT DAWN, SEAGULLS SWOOPED OVER THE CITY OF LONDON IN A D-DAY MOCK ATTACK AS CORRUPTION ON A MAJOR SCALE WAS EXPOSED. FTSE FALLS 500 NYSE ROCKS AND DOW JONES COLLAPSES.

However, there was little said about transactions that had taken place abroad and I remembered that I had promised myself that I would look into the Anderson case 'if I ever had a chance'. Well I certainly had a chance now but I was still not sure how to proceed to uncover TLT and the 'secret' code. Uncle Wilfrid had been in the Navy and knew something about codes, and he had said it was likely that TLT used a 'semiotic' system, but that meant nothing to me at the time.

We had done our bit to make sure that St Hylda would 'never be forgotten' and I felt good, but 'not that good' so I decided to ring Gordon Bird to see if he might think of something in a kilt to cheer me up. I began to smile.

Part Two
Gordon's Story

Foreword

In **Part One,** Elda Whitby narrated her own experiences of love and betrayal in a complex world in which illegal property speculation continued to thrive. In doing so, she had to face uncomfortable truths about herself as well as others, and even risk her own life as she tried to distinguish friend from foe.

In **Part Two,** now it is Gordon Bird's turn to continue the tale. You may remember that Elda had only met him a few times, but after the debacle over Uncle Wilfrid's death, she had lost trust in Luke and, as a knee jerk reaction, telephoned Gordon to 'see if he might cheer her up'. Here is his story.

Chapter One
The Bird Man

I hadn't seen or heard from Elda or any of my friends from college in a very long time, so it was a real and very pleasant surprise to get a phone call from her suggesting that we should meet up.

Elda had mentioned me briefly as her 'Angus' from college and I am that Gordon Bird. I have learnt to live with the 'Bird Man' soubriquet for a very long time, well before the famous 1962 film *The Bird Man of Alcatraz*, in which Burt Lancaster played the part of the infamous Robert Stroud incarcerated there in 1909. Stroud found some kind of peace and redemption after he had 'adopted' and cared for wild sparrows in his cell.

I didn't plan on going to prison but I did share his love of ornithology, ending up in 1950 as a lecturer in Environmental Studies at Birmingham University and it was there that I had met her.

Being a 'Whitby', she engaged her friends (and me sometimes) with tales from a distant Anglo-Saxon past in which St Hylda at Whitby Abbey ruled the roost (we used to joke about that) with dawn birds at her beck and call when she needed them. Elda enjoyed our environmental studies especially when we had a 'field' trip to Dartmoor but she always had more questions than answers (maybe the mark of a good student). For example, there was so much virtual wasteland that she couldn't understand why it was not populated or farmed, and answers about enclosures and land acquisitions by the Duke of this or that on a worldwide basis only served to irritate her even more. She even mentioned a case of a Professor Anderson that she and her Uncle had investigated back in the UK. "It seems that she acquired land in Africa as part of a dubious property deal, with an obscure company called TLT," she said. "But I'll track her down one day." And with that, she laughed and I loved her for it. However, it was not all work and no play for her and everyone knew that she fancied Father Luke like mad, so you might say that some thought she was a bit strange, not to say weird. After all, priests were supposed to be 'off the menu' at our college and birds didn't swoop on demand, did they? Anyway, I liked her, and she liked me as we danced at our college discos as she laughed and laughed and as I twirled around in my Campbell kilt with sporran a wobbling.

"Do it again, Angus!" (Her pet name for me) she would cry, "Go on. Do it again." Yes, we had some good times but I never saw Luke at the discos nor afterwards when we all spit up and made our separate ways. I didn't see Elda again either, that is until I received a phone call out of the blue from her asking to meet me for coffee. She said that she hoped I might cheer her up, 'sporran fashion' and of course, I agreed.

That coffee led to many more and numerous outings of a platonic nature until a weekend in Bournemouth for the CBSO 'Elgar' weekend. We stayed at The Hotel Miramar close to the pier with separate rooms as usual, bidding each other good night in the lobby. It had been a great performance so I was soon asleep but woken up with a start at 6 am when there was a tap on the door. I quickly donned a bath robe and there was Elda in a HERS version of my HIS robe. Her hair was damp and she smelt of honeysuckle. I couldn't decide if she had just had a shower or had been out in the rain because, as I looked out of the window, it was raining 'cats and dogs' (they say) but this rain was populated by dozens of squalling seagulls, some of whom swooped dangerously close to my balcony. Elda was very excited.

"Can you see them? Can you hear them?" she said, leading me closer to the window. "It's the dawn birds! At least they can be trusted when you need them and I do need them, oh, how I need them, but most of all, I need you now, Angus. Please tell me you feel the same and show me that you do." I smiled without hesitation as our bathrobes fell simultaneously to the floor. We made love for most of the day in my room at the hotel, ignoring the frequent room service calls from the corridor outside, but all too soon, we had to travel home. I was expecting some unwelcoming news and I was soon proven right when I opened the clutch of letters on the doormat that awaited me, and my heart sank. One of the letters had no stamp but was franked MOD IMPORTANT DOCUMENTS and I knew at once what it was and sighed, "Bad news, Angus?" Elda asked.

The letter was a request, no, a demand that I attend the Sandhurst Military Academy for initial training for my National Service in two weeks. I was being fast-tracked, it stated but I knew that it would be 'square bashing' away from home anyway. Two weeks ago, I had been told about the death of my friend Mike as he flew a mission as part of a squadron of Meteors in Aden. Other mates were Alan in Malaya, as well as John in Suez and Peter in Germany all sent to 'Empire' hot spots as part of their National Service, and now it would be my turn. I felt helpless at that moment. Where would I be posted, and I wondered if Elda would still want me so I decided that I had to tell her everything. I was very relieved when, after I had finished, she snuggled and said, "I hope that they make you wear your kilt on parade with me."

I had to laugh and it might have been just as it used to be if it wasn't for the spectre of National Service looming. With cut backs and shortages, the MOD had cut training short. Sandhurst came and went and dreary Aldershot came and went as well, until one day I got my 'marching orders' (as it were). I opened my second MOD envelope and called out to Elda who was in the bath, but now appearing in a haze of steam as she kissed my forehead. "Where the heck is Gil-Gil?" I said, "cos that's where I've been sent to."

She suddenly looked very serious and backed away, picking up a copy of *the Times* from table before handing it to me. I read the headline and this is what it said.

Massacre at Gil Gil./ Mau Mau overrun British Garrison in Rift Valley Kenya.

Army personnel and civilians have been reported dead, including 12 British officers of the KAR (The King's African Rifles) and at least 50 of their African troopers. Equally tragic though was the murder of two defenceless European families, namely Hugh Evans, a local farmer, with his wife and daughter and Jeremy Jones from Tenby in South Wales, now a doctor, with his 12-year-old son. Both families were horribly mutilated. The Mau Mau left more than a hundred dead bodies behind before they disappeared into the bush. The troops followed and killed all they could find in their villages including women and children, all classified as 'terrorists', it was said.

I didn't know what to say to re-assure Elda because I was rather worried but she was way ahead of me. "These fracases come and go," she said, "Like as not the KAR (King's African Rifles) and your lot will be back in no time with a few more bodies in bags." She didn't like war, but most of all, she didn't like injustice and she thought that it was time for Britain to pull out of Kenya as well as her colonies elsewhere. She was one of those women who 'walked the walk', as well as 'talking the talk', so I suppose I was not too surprised when she said that she was coming with me. "I knew you'd get your call up sooner or later," she said, "So I joined the Queen Alexandra's Nursing Brigade some months back so that I'd be ready to go with you when the time came to go to whatever miserable spot in the Empire they sent you to." She smiled, knowing that she had achieved a remarkable victory by demonstrating her love and support for me whilst damning the Empire to Hell.

It would be churlish not to be very thankful for a short break and for our journey from King George Dock in London to Mombasa aboard the P&O liner Stratheden, although it was essentially a troop ship with armaments and supplies on board. There was a section for women but that didn't stop Angus from finding a way for 'his' way, I'm glad to say. Then, as we pulled into Mombasa at dawn on that Sunday morning after 10 days at sea, Elda pointed at the sky as a horde of seagulls swooped to greet us. "Look!" she cried. "Look! It's the dawn birds. We'll be safe now!"

Chapter Two
White Mischief

Safe or not, Elda and I could not forget that we were entering into a warzone, and not just any old war. This war or 'struggle for independence' (as characterised by the Mau Mau) exposed brutality of a kind that people had hoped to forget about after the recent War that had been over for less than ten years. At that time, papers had been full of the Holocaust in Europe and the forced death marches under Japanese control in Asia. These boils had been lanced with the Atom bombs at Hiroshima and Nagasaki, as well as the Nuremburg Trials, but had we won the war only to sink into a kind of bestiality all over again? I knew Elda's views on the matter but I was to be a soldier, so would this mean that 'anything goes' once I'd signed on the dotted line? What is more, I was not a volunteer but a conscripted man so did I still have to toe any old line that the brigadier drew in the sand? Simply put, could a soldier afford to have any principles at all? I suspected that the answer was no, and this answer was attested to by the many 'conscientious objectors' who were shot by our own side, during World War One, for desertion or refusing to serve. To ease my conscience a little, I decided to look at some history to prove that there were some causes worth fighting, killing and dying for, such as Nazism, but were the 'White Highlands Settlements' of Kenya one of them?

Elda noticed that I looked worried, and one day she gave me the 1941 book called *White Mischief* which was a non-fiction novel about fun and games in an outpost of Empire, beset with immorality and corruption in the 1920s, or the three As Elda put it, namely Aristocracy, Alcohol and Adultery. "Read that," she said, "and then tell me who killed the Earl of Errol, or perhaps the question should be who didn't? So many had motives, and all with their own reasons, maybe then you'll see what we are up against. It's not the Mau Mau but the legacy of a very rotten colonialism that's at the root of it all."

I knew what she was getting at, as the sense of a British Empire that 'ruled the waves (and the world)' was prevalent throughout 'our' territories and beyond and no less so (even more so) in Kenya as it became part of the 'Scramble for Africa' between the UK and French with peripheral activity by Portugal, Germany and Belgium to mention but a few. India had shown the way in Victoria's hey-day and that example was the ambition of many a governor general or district commissioner. PM Balfour's solution for so-called legal settlement in 1902 was the sequestration of land wherever title seemed dubious, and a Crown Colony Ordinance was announced that specified British or Irish settlement only for large tracts of the best farmland. As might be expected British Diplomacy tried a legal ruse, namely that the British would lease the land or buy the land from the Kikuyu. Details of lease or buy were unclear and it was this misunderstanding, amongst other things, that led to the bloody Mau Mau revolt in 1952 and the reason that I was there. I had already decided to make the best of it, but there was little of that to be had, as I had to lead punitive raids into seemingly peaceful villages with every black figure a target as a suspected terrorist, including children. Sometimes, we captured a man or woman carrying a weapon (we even called the Panga a weapon) and such persons would be sent for trial and often hanged, 'according to the law'.

This was the state of affairs in which I found myself and if it wasn't for Elda, I think I'd have gone mad. Fortunately after about a three-month tour of duty, I got a weekend off and suggested that we went to Lake Nakuru for a break. She was delighted. I loved her when she showed so much emotion over seemingly trivial matters but she carried her heart on her sleeve and covered me with kisses. "Oh, thank you, Angus," she said with a smile, "Thank you, thank you, just you, me and the birds then. What could be more idyllic?"

I didn't tell her that I could do without the birds because she snuggled up so close, then closer and closer yet until we drifted off to sleep ready for our adventure the next day. Unfortunately I couldn't settle down and pictures of flamingos persisted in my imagination so much so that I got up and composed a poem for Elda and her birds.

Well we can all fly, can't we? I mean, not in the sky like those flying flamingos, because we don't have wings, do we? At least I don't, and those who think they do can come down to earth with a bang, like that Greek fly half called Icarus of whom you may have heard, who thought he was a fly (I mean a bird), What's more, you don't need wings to fly like those big pink birds and pelicans up high. They all fly around and end up where they started, back in the lake where it all began,

even, it is said, original man. But a book once told me
something true. It said 'if you would fly, spread your wings,
take off and be you'. All you need is love like a dove with a
coo, not like those birds knee deep in Lake Nakuru goo.

I was now sleepy and snuggled down hoping Elda would like my poem.

It was soon dawn and Elda was bouncing up and down on the bed, shaking me into some state of life. "Look. Listen," she cried out, "It's the dawn birds, they have found us and everything will be fine from now on. Hug me, Angus, I love you, I love you." I hugged her tight but something of a premonition came over me as I realised that I would soon have to return to duty with all that that entailed. Furthermore, I knew that Elda had attended social gatherings with some of the senior Asian and African leaders outside Nairobi and I prayed that she knew what she was doing. I also knew that she had made enquiries about Mrs (Professor) Anderson who was now an important JP in the area and a director of the company TLT that Elda had mentioned.

Meanwhile, we shuffled back into bed and I told her to shut her eyes while I read my poem. When I had finished, I could see that her eyes were glistening. "That's beautiful, Angus." she said, "And so are you. Let's take a boat out on the lake and pretend we are flamingos and show them we can float as well as fly."

That was a lovely day and then I sprang to my next surprise. It was to be a few days at the famous Treetops Hotel where Princess Elizabeth, as she then was, had stayed with Prince Philip, and it was there on 6 February 1952 that they heard that George V1 had died. It was barely six months ago, so there was still an air of fascination about the place and the events that took place there. Treetops is close to the Aberdare mountains and in the foothills of Mount Kenya, so it was a change of scenery as well. We were very impressed but I sensed that Elda was perturbed, "How the other half lives," she kept saying, but even she could not deny the unique structure which was built as a tree house with a viewing platform (a machan) from which wild game could be viewed and shot. The idea of a tree house was a rather romantic story in itself having been built in 1932 by Major Eric Sherbrook Walker for his wife, Lady Bettie.

Unfortunately as I write this, some years later I have to report that the Mau Mau burnt it down in 1954 so we had got there just in time.

I was soon back to military duties chasing an almost invisible foe who knew the territory much better than we did, and we were also aware that the UK government were in talks with Jomo Kenyatta, the Kikuyu leader with links to the Mau Mau. In this regard, we, the National Service recruits, suspected that we were in effect a 'holding' operation only and that it would soon be all over.

Then one day there was a knock on the door and before I could get to it, Elda was on her feet. "Don't forget, I will always love you, my lovely Angus," she said before stepping to the door and opening it. I was right behind her in the half light as I saw my Troop Sergeant 'Jock' Lawrence and two sturdy African troopers from the KAR (King's African Rifles) waiting patiently.

"Good morning, Jock," I said, "Now, what's this all about then?"

Jock looked somewhat discomfited and shuffled a bit before he replied. "So sorry to disturb you, sir and ma'am, but we've come to ask if Ms Whitby would kindly come with us to the police station to answer a few questions. And one more thing, we need her to come with us now and please bring an overnight bag."

I wanted to punch him on the nose but Elda was as calm as could be. "Thank you, Jock," she said with a smile, "Gordon, please go indoors and bring me that blue travel bag by the bed. I've had it ready for ages." I did as she asked and handed it to her on the doorstep with a shaking hand. She grasped it firmly and said, "Look, Angus. Just look up at the sky right now." I did as she asked, and as dawn was breaking, I could just about see a flock of gulls approaching at a rapid pace before wheeling around and around. "There you are," said Elda triumphantly, "Right on time. Don't worry about me, Gordon, I'm in safe hands now, and I'll be home very soon," and with that she walked to the Land Rover that awaited her.

This was a most optimistic point of view because shortly after arrival at the police station, she was transported with other 'suspects' to the infamous prison at Eldoret in the Uasin Gishu basin far away from the Kikuyu land. This was right at the northernmost point of the Great Trek of the Boers from the Transvaal that occurred from 1836 and was sustained during the Boer Wars up to 1902. This idea of a new living space for the 'voortrekkers' persisted throughout the next century resulting in the racist apartheid regime in South Africa and to whom the Eldoret 'Boers' continued to look for support. So in that particular 'Happy Valley' of the Uasin Gishu basin and Eldoret, it was the Afrikaans who held sway, albeit under British control and the native Luo or Nandi tribes remained totally subservient to their white masters such as the Van Trasks, the Van Diedens or Meintjes families. It was a good place to have a prison, miles from nowhere with potentially hostile natives in the bush and I was not allowed to visit, being considered a potential security risk myself. I was at my wit's end, so I decided to ask for a transfer for us both back to 'Dear Ol Blighty', as I put it. "We'll do what we can for you," said the Officer Commanding, "But Ms Whitby must make her own way, that is, if she gets a pardon for assisting the enemy. Of course, it would be different if you were married."

This seemed like a godsend to me and I arranged for Elda to receive the good news but I was taken aback by her response by letter. It read:

Dear Gordon,

You know that I love you but I will not be blackmailed in this way. We'll just have to be patient.

I would have done anything to get us out of there but perhaps she was right about being patient. *I could save my salary and pay for her travel*, I thought but that was before I learnt that she had been sentenced to twenty years for sedition. I cried and cried but what could I do? My solution was to get a permit to go and see her and this was granted, and a bit later, I arrived at the Delamere Hotel just outside the town. I then stayed overnight with an appointment to see her in the morning, but I was in for a big surprise.

The next morning, I was sitting in a comfortable chair in the bar as Dawn broke when I spied a familiar figure walking through the swing doors and heading directly for me. He stopped and smiled, "Hello, Gordon, how are things?" he said. It was Luke, <u>Father</u> Luke, because once again, he was in his full priestly costume and shiny white collar.

I stood and held out my hand, "Luke," I said as we shook hands firmly, "Dear Luke; after all this time. So what brings you to Eldoret then?"

He explained that he was now an assistant bishop for the Uasin Gishu region and was kept very busy with his work in the community. "But that's not why I'm here," he said, "I've actually come to officiate at a wedding, that's my prerogative as visiting Bishop."

"That's great," I said, "So who is the lucky couple?"

Now he paused, then he gave me a broad grin and said, "Yours, silly, you and Elda. It's all arranged."

I couldn't decide whether to laugh or to cry so I walked to the windows and looked to see the dawn birds circling. It seemed that Elda had changed her mind. Luke had worked a miracle.

Part Three
Luke's Story

Foreword

You have heard from Elda and Gordon about how we had met up and spent some time in the past, so now it's my turn to declare my own different perspective.

My name is Luke Collins, sometimes Father Luke, an ordained priest in the Roman Catholic Faith. I say sometimes because my involvement with the Church has not always been an easy one; but then I don't think I expected that it would be. Magical moments vied with very depressing days as I struggled with the contradictions of obedience and personal autonomy that I found as I made my way in the world.

Chapter One
Once in Love

I'm Luke Collins and I had met Elda and Gordon at Newman College Birmingham University where I was a pastoral adviser and lecturer in Faith Studies and I think that I have loved her from the start. They were both students and we seemed to get on well enough but I did become aware that Elda often looked at me intently, even when I was in conversation with others. When I looked back, she always treated me with an almost provocative smile and I had to turn away. Susie noticed and, one day on leaving our seminar, she turned to me and said, "She don't half fancy you, sir," before she scurried off down the corridor with a laugh. This was unfortunate to say the least because I valued my reputation as that kind of teacher who didn't mess with students, so I had to suppress my own feelings. I must admit though that I was drawn to her in a very 'real' way, academically, emotionally, spiritually and yes, even physically but, being a Jesuit, I was aware that self-denial could bring a spiritual uplift. However I was also finding out that human nature has to have 'her' say as well.

Wasn't it St Augustine who said, "Lord, make me pure but not yet"? And I know exactly how he felt. In Part Two,

Gordon told us how it was that I was able to marry him and Elda in Eldoret prison many years later, so I think it's incumbent on me now to fill in the gaps to explain how it came about.

It's a very long story but the first gap covers the years after we all left the university and I became an RE/History teacher at a Birmingham RC secondary school, having ceased any contact with them or any other students for that matter. I soon got into the swing of things and even spent time in the music department as an unofficial aide to the Head of Music. He was a charismatic, larger than life individual named Alistair Dark-Brown. Of course, this amused the 'kids' as actually he was a very white Anglo-Saxon from Grimsby but I liked him very much. He taught me about the classical and romantic composers from Bach to Berlioz and I tried to interest him in Jelly Roll Morton's *Red-Hot Peppers* as well as the alto sax of Art Pepper. We became very close inside that rather narrow wavelength that friends share; a wavelength that others were not privy to in matters such as personal preferences and even feelings. I'd say that we had become very good friends indeed but that's as far as it went but once again, as with Elda, I sensed that he 'fancied' me. "I could easily love you, Luke," he said one day, "don't you love me a little?" I assured him that I did love him but not in that way. He smiled and murmured, "Well there's always Oscar, I suppose." I laughed because I had seen him and his friend out socially many times. However it did not cross my mind at the time that he and Oscar were indeed having a gay affair. To cap it all, my 'special' friendship with Alistair was soon to be called to a halt as others had misconstrued the very nature of it.

On top of this, I was called to see the deputy head one day and she told me that there had been a complaint by two girls in class 2B. "They say that you have told them that you like boys as much as girls," she said with a rather withering look.

I must admit that I was speechless for a moment before I replied. "Well, miss," I said "It's true that I don't have favourites if that's what you mean, and what's wrong with that?"

Now she gazed at me pityingly. "Don't be naïve, Luke," she said, "I'm here to tell you that the matter will be raised at the next governor's meeting and if you want my advice, you'll steer clear of Alistair for the time being. His case will also be held next week. Thank you, please see yourself out."

At last it dawned on me that Alistair and I were under scrutiny for homosexual tendencies, if not proven behaviour; and the Church doesn't like that sort of thing, does it? I nearly packed my bag but decided to meet up with Alistair as usual. "Sorry, yes, they've got me," he said, "Seen holding hands with Oscar; bad boy. Resign now, no choice." I shook his hand, said goodbye and handed in my notice the very next day. I decided to retrain with the OU and completed a website accounting diploma in no time at all, with letters after my name. I was now Luke Collins, WA. Fortunately I was able to find some private students and also to become an examiner for Edexcel, which was a foremost examining board at the time. I bought a small house near Yapton in West Sussex and was able to commute up and down on Southern Railway from Barnham to Brighton, Gatwick, Chichester, and even London. So imagine my surprise when, out of the blue, and on an especially cold and frosty morning, I met Elda in the station coffee bar. It seemed that fate had taken a hand and I was grateful to her for it.

I think that Elda has told you in Part One about our whirlwind romance when we threw caution to the wind and allowed our feelings full-reign. At last she said it to me, "I love you, Luke, but you have always known that, haven't you?" No answer to that was necessary as I gathered her in my arms and laid her gently down on the bed. Our nights were so loving in the most romantic of ways because that is what 'turned her on', as she would say, and it certainly suited me. However, no matter if we had spent a quiet or a vigorous night, she was always awake at dawn, nudging me to come and see. "Look, Luke, it's the dawn birds again," she would say, "Aren't they beautiful?"

"It's you who's beautiful." I would reply as I nuzzled her bare back as she stood at the window. Yes, those days were idyllic because we lived close-by and were able to see each other regularly even though we both had jobs to do. She was also a teacher at a small primary school, but much of her time was spent as a 'Guardian' of the ancient society of St Hylda that had dedicated itself to land reform and she and Uncle Wilfrid were very close to a major exposure of fraud on a wide-scale and my clumsy intervention didn't help.

"How could I ever trust you again?" she had said, "I loved you and you deceived me. Please go." I didn't know what to say as I left with my heart truly broken.

Chapter Two
Still in Love

After my debacle with Elda, I knew that it was time for me to pick myself up and renew my work as a Jesuit 'in the community' as a 'clerk regular'. This is the name given to Jesuits who may, temporarily or permanently, be outside the Holy Orders. Adhering to my vows has never been easy and I generally only gave myself a score of one out of three, namely poverty. The others of obedience and chastity were much harder. However, there was a fourth that came to my rescue at this time namely a Jesuit 'special obedience to the Pope with regard to missions', and it was here that I thought I might make amends for the past as well add a valid contribution to the future, but how and where?

Fortunately I did not have to wait long before I espied a small advert in the *Jesuit Times* stating that missions in Kenya were very short of teachers capable and willing to serve the purpose of God and the community. I applied and was soon on my way to Mombasa on the SS Arcadia. I didn't know too much about Kenya at the time but I felt that I was truly in God's hands and that He had a purpose for me in the world. I said my prayers at night as usual and then found myself adding, "and God bless Elda". This was the first time I had done so as I began to realise how much I missed her. My instructions were to make my way via Nairobi to the northern tip of the country bordering Uganda, to a small town called Eldoret where accommodation had been arranged. I was to meet with the neighbouring parish priest from Kitale who would give me details and I was looking forward to that as my Peugeot 404 Taxi pulled up at some very formidable gates with an armed guard on both sides.

My driver spoke for a while and then drove into an idyllic village setting with bungalows of white with red tile roofs on every corner, all with green and well-watered lawns in what was otherwise a very dry atmosphere. He drew up at number twenty and said, "Here we are, Bwana, here is your Shamba." He took my bags out of the boot and handed me a key as he left. "Quahiri Bwana," he said, and even my poor Swahili knew that this meant goodbye. The taxi then took off at a very fast rate as I was dumped on my doorstep. I was alone, maybe for the very first time in my life.

I looked around my new surroundings that seemed to be entirely separate from the town of Eldoret that we had driven through, and they did not seem to stack up with my idea of the African 'community' that I was there for. Be that as it may, I found that I was warmly welcomed by most of the British expatriates who occupied senior positions in the company but I'd say that I was barely tolerated by others. This gated habitat was, in fact, a microcosm of much that was wrong with Kipling's idea of the *White Man's Burden*, that he had seen as valid and beneficial; yet here we had the British at odds with the Africans, the Africans at odds with them both as well as tribal rivalries, and then our Asian friends at odds with each other over Indian partition.

It was not clear how this small settlement had been created and by whom, but I made it my business to look up the original and current trustees. In 1902, following the Balfour Land Apportionment Acts, it was of course Lord Delamere and others from the British aristocracy, but in more recent years, they had been increased by some from the legal and other professions. It was then that I noticed a familiar name, that of a certain Professor Mrs Anderson, late of Chichester in the UK. I immediately thought of Elda's determination to find out more about the circumstances in which Professor Anderson had been 'persuaded' to relinquish her title to her English estate and then to emigrate to Africa. Some transaction documents were attached to her application to be a trustee, but strangely, they were not in English or Swahili but a hybrid of both. The format seemed to be the 'semiotic' principle in which a meaning is interpreted from the results of an action, or more accurately, an implication but not the action itself. Both sender and receiver would need to have identical interpretations to decode a message so that no confusion was possible. I knew about this method of coding in which actual transaction details were masked in this way, but it was usually in the church or the military and I wondered why the TLT documents did so.

Elda had said that if she ever got the chance, she would try to find out, 'in memory of Uncle Wilfrid'. So here was my opportunity to help her if I ever got the chance to do so. Perhaps I might be able to make additional amends for my clumsiness back then. Unfortunately, we had lost touch since the wedding but I knew that they had gone to Naivasha, so I asked for permission to see them and it was granted.

I had accepted my 'lot' and was determined to make the best of it and, as if to help me along, I was awakened at dawn by the arrival of two ring-necked doves on my veranda making a quiet billing and cooing that immediately reminded me of Elda so far away. *Not the dawn birds*, I thought, *but love birds, and how things might have been so different.* I wanted to share the moment and began a quite ordinary conversation with her *as if she was there.* "Look Elda, here they are again. Bill and Coo," I said, "Do you think they're in love?"

By now, I had a houseboy, Ondago, and he said that this was the first time he had seen the doves in Eldoret. "You see them in Kitale," he said, "But not here. You very blessed," and I agreed. I hoped to see them for myself on the following day as I was to drive (I now had a VW Beetle) to Kitale to see Father Matthew and as I drove, I noticed the many African houses on the roadside, and I wished that I had been given one.

That profound wish was confirmed a few weeks later when, despite all the security precautions on my estate, I had to deal with a latenight intruder. This possibility had not entered my mind, and in fact, our bungalows had a security system that should have worked. The arrangement was that, on going to bed, the interconnecting door between living and sleeping quarters would be locked, and all the windows in the bedrooms were heavily barred following recent emergencies with the Mau Mau, so security in the sleeping area was ensured. However, the builders had not accounted for a naïve priest in his first weeks hearing a noise and deciding to deal with it. I was awakened at about 4 am when I heard something from the living area and so I walked down the corridor to see what it was. I planned to open the connecting door with the key with which I had locked it a few hours earlier but it wasn't there. Impossible! Had I taken it back to the bedroom by mistake? But no, it was not there either when I checked so I went back to the door. It was then that I saw it, on a sheet of paper slotted under the door from the other side. I think I must have been rather sleepy and not very sensible, because I just decided to pick it up, open the door and walk through and this decision could have cost me my life. It was moonlight and rather gloomy as I approached the curtain in the archway that separated the dining and living areas, but before I got there, the curtain launched towards me with a figure inside. I backed away but both soon disappeared out of the window and I was alone, but safe, again. I hurried out of the house to my neighbours, Jon and Jane Scott, and they telephoned the police.

"Why didn't you ring the alarm?" asked Jane.

I looked blank and in that time honoured phrase just said, "What alarm?" Well, it transpired that all bedrooms had an alarm switch but nobody had told me. That night I slept badly, interrupting my Hail Mary's with an appeal to Elda to come and save me. "It's been a bad day," I said, "How are you getting on, my darling? I miss you terribly and can't wait to see you very soon."

There was no reply but it didn't matter because I hadn't expected one. "Talk to you tomorrow," I said.

The MD called me the next day to see if I was OK and his question was as irritating as Jane's. "What did you think that large button in the bedroom was for then?" he said.

Next day I asked Ondago if anything was missing and he said, "Only food, Bwana, meat and some bread and chocolate." I felt very sad to think that someone had risked so much for so little when I would have gladly given him what he needed. But this was Africa, not rural Sussex and I had to learn fast. Another steep learning curve was delivered to me a few days later when Father Matthew brought me a letter from the bishop asking me to travel to Nairobi. My job would be to comfort the prisoners in Nairobi gaol following recent Mau Mau activities. Shortages of staff at the prison and within the Church meant that extra hands were needed to administer God's grace, confession and communion, if requested. This seemed totally in keeping with my duties as a Jesuit so I was happy to take another Peugeot 404 south. We arrived at dawn and (I know you know what I'm going to say but it's true nonetheless) with night-time turning to day, the sky above the gaol was filled with those squawking unfriendly gulls that I had seen many times before, and I knew that this time it was a warning.

It was early days for the Mau Mau but two factors united them. Firstly the thorny question of the 1902 land settlements but also the assassination of the senior chief Waruhiu following which riots had begun on a major scale. The new governor, Sir Evelyn Baring, had introduced a state of emergency in 1952, ergo more riots. The death toll rose and ruthless British military action followed, leading to 80.00 Kikuyu in gaol by the end of the conflict, with at least 1000 executions and although I did not know it at the time, my job would be to attend quite a few of them. I suppose it was all very well for me, a newcomer to have principles but by now the Mau Mau thrived on terror. Members had to swear oaths and there were secret initiations and mutilations for any African who refused to join. Nevertheless, that first day in the prison yard made me sick. There was no dignity, none at all, as 4x4 prisoners mounted the platform, a noose was added and then they dropped through the trapdoor. The drop was only a few feet so most were strangled in great pain as the next 4x4 lined up. My job was to offer comfort, wasn't it, but in the many weeks that I stood there, only one lady asked for a blessing as she said, "Bless me, Father, for I have sinned. I would like you to have this small gift to remember me." She handed me a package and the next moment she was in heaven. That evening I opened it and saw that it was a small prayer book with her name, *To Fatuma Smith on your confirmation*. My hands were shaking as I put it in my bag and I still have it to this day. I tried to carry on but found that I was grateful that no one asked for a blessing and I knew that this was wrong as well.

Eventually I asked the bishop and the prison governor to release me and they did by offering me another related job. This was to accompany many of the less hardened criminals to the prison at Eldoret close to my 'shamba'. This suited me down to the ground and I was very grateful, but when they showed me the list, you could have knocked me down with a dawn bird feather because there on that long list was the very familiar name of Elda Whitby. I was curious, of course, and made it my business to find out how she might be pardoned or paroled. I was told that there was no possibility but I just refused to accept such a decision. "It would be different if she was married," said the Governor and that's how the idea came into my head.

"Well, she will be," I said bluntly and I think that Gordon has told you the rest. "I'm going to make sure she damn well is," And with that, I left the room. It only remained for me to find Gordon, Second Lieutenant Bird and tell him.

"She'll never agree," he said, but I wouldn't accept that either. I was *still in love with Elda*, and this would be my moment to prove it.

"Just give her some excuse and I'll do the rest." I said. A week later, we accompanied the prisoners to the gaol in Eldoret and arranged to take Elda to one side to tell her the news. "I've come to marry you," I said rather huskily, "You and Gordon. Please, take his hand." She did, they kissed and I smiled. It was one of the most beautiful moments of my life and one that I would turn to again and again.

Now I returned to my shamba with a feeling of contentment. I sat on the veranda throughout the night and waited for 'Bill and Coo' to come to me for their feed of millet grain. Ondago had told me that the doves had not come to Eldoret in the past because of the peregrine falcons who built their nests in the trees that surrounded our small estate. Yet now Bill and Coo were oblivious to their threat as was I. "Thank you, St Elda," I said on their behalf as I took a sip of lager.

Such bliss was not to last for long, however, as I received another letter from the Holy See to take up a position 'of great importance' in Tanzania, following President Nyerere's recent baptism as a Roman Catholic with the name of 'Julius', following his translations of Shakespeare's *Merchant of Venice* and *Caesar*. The Pope's advisers did not know which way he would turn, as he was also known to have sympathetic 'communist' tendencies, a suggestion that was anathema to Pius X11. It was also known that Nyerere had important family links with local religious traditions, and some felt that this was too close to a potential Mau Mau scenario. Against this negative opinion was the fact that the Pope had been trying to re-establish Catholicism in Africa after World War Two and so he welcomed an important ally. Where it would lead, no one knew at the time, but if actions speak louder than words, his policies were soon evident in 'nationalisation' and trade links with China. I rather liked his stance and thought it in keeping with Catholic teaching with one eye on the underprivileged and the other on faith. "What do you think, dearest?" I asked Elda in my dreams on more than one occasion. No answer but I knew that she would have approved. I had grown to admire his single-minded conviction to do what is right, and I only hoped that I might be able to emulate him one day. In the meantime I still had a job to do but what was it? I had had no guidance, only that the Holy Father wanted to revive the Church but how was I to do it?

I had heard of a nun who ran a shelter for homeless girls in Dar so I decided to do the same for boys, thus taking orphans off the street and showing them the beauty of a life in Christ as well. Now this was an honourable task I felt, but suspicion was rife here in Dar as it had been in Kenya, and throughout most of British Colonial Africa for that matter and I couldn't be expected to put that right, could I? Then on my knees in prayer one night, I think that I found the answer and I'm sure that it was Elda who guided me. In my prayers, a voice seemed to say, "Just go to see the President and ask him what to do." I thought a night's sleep would do me good, and when I woke up in the morning, I knew that I had been given a sign and a direction.

My meeting with Nyerere was very short just after I had celebrated Mass. He reminded me of Gandhi as he would not allow me to bring him tea but insisted on doing that himself. "I have heard of your idea for a boys' sanctuary," he said, "Tanzania is grateful so please help as you can while you are here. I have grand plans for my country but there will be resistance," he said, "and not just from European vested interests but from my own followers too. You see, people do not like change in their lives, but when it is inevitable, we have to let it flow around our basic beliefs rather than to change them. Our beliefs are simply those that keep us human after all." He smiled, a most engaging smile, and I remembered this short homily later when he failed to deliver collective farming. I prayed that he would recover and sure enough, he even accelerated his ambitions for social equality and peaceful change.

As he said *Quahiri* and wished me well, he added one small item that I had hardly considered. "There's trouble brewing in Southern Rhodesia," he said, "they will need you more than we do. The time for talk is nearly over and we'll soon have another war on our hands in East Africa and they will need good people like you." I was flattered of course but did not expect to hear much more about his prognosis. Wrong again!

I wasn't to know it, of course, but he was right, and after some happy years in Bagamoyo, I was suddenly given an assignment to go to Rhodesia on another 'mission' for His Holiness via the bishop. "The country is falling apart," he said, "we can't do much from here and there is only one man, Joshua Nkomo, who might be influential enough to avert violence even if Smith's threats of UDI are carried out. We can't approach him direct but we have a contact that you must get in touch with. His name is Joseph Gondo and we'll fix it so you can meet him privately at first. Nkomo is a difficult man to pin down so it might take a bit of time but be patient and maybe you'll get lucky."

Unlike Tanzania but very much like Kenya, I knew that Rhodesia was a fragmented society with the extra dimension of two major tribes vying for control as Prime Minister Smith continued to apply pressure for UDI, his preferred option, that of a 'Unilateral Declaration' nearly ready to go. I'm not entirely sure that our bishop knew 'his' Africa because although, on the one hand there was indeed Nkomo of the Ndebele in Bulawayo, I also knew that there were rival tribal forces in the country, not least those led by Robert Mugabe with the Shona in Salisbury. They were allies against Smith, but sometimes sworn tribal enemies and I thought I might have to negotiate with both.

"Go see him as soon as you can," said the Bishop, "but remember that a 'mission' is all his Holiness asks, not a miracle, although I must admit that one would help."

I desperately wanted to see Elda and Gordon before I left, and soon my application for a break was granted and I also received an invitation to Naivasha for a very 'Happy Event' as Elda put it. This would be a diversion from my planned route from Dar es Salaam to Salisbury, but I thought that it was well worth it and when I arrived, I knew that I was right.

Gordon greeted me like a brother and Elda smothered me in kisses, barely containing her excitement. "Come in, come in," she said, "Look! We have a present for you." She led me by the hand into a small area at the back of the lounge stooping to pick up a bundle from a small cot. "Here she is," she said triumphantly, "this is Lou-Lou or Lucy to you, and this, my little precious, is your godfather and 'honorary uncle', Luke."

I took the bundle gently and said, 'Hi, Lou-Lou, how are you-you?" and we all laughed. Apparently I had been designated godfather at her christening the day before and I felt immensely privileged. Once more, I had a loving 'family' to share my life with, albeit for a very short time as I only had a week before I had to travel south. That time we spent on the shores of the lake, watching the pelicans gliding down like B52 bombers but with beaks open, trawling for fish. I held baby Lou-Lou every day and could barely give her back when it was time to go, but that time arrived all too soon. Elda was in tears and Gordon a most stoic Scotsman, as I took my leave in a familiar Peugeot 404 to head toward Nkomo's home in Bulawayo. I must admit that I left with a heavy heart, as I knew that Gordon still had many months to go in his National Service, but he assured me that they planned to buy the farm that they occupied in Naivasha and to settle down to family life, but the situation remained volatile as we both knew.

"You will look after them, won't you, Luke? I mean if anything happens to me," he said.

"Don't be silly," I replied, "I'm in more danger than you are on my way to Rhodesia, but if they ever need me, I will be there for them. I give you my solemn promise."

Chapter Three
Always in Love with Amy

Shortly after I arrived in Salisbury, I was met by Joseph Gondo and given a few tips about Nkomo. "He's very clever and very committed to African rule here. He has a Trade Union background so is very well aware of the tensions between employers and workers. Be polite and most of all, tell him that you agree with his position on land reform and that will get him on your side."

Now I had to get down to business with the main man, but apart from Joseph's tips, I didn't know where to start. In other words, what exactly was my mission? I'd had very little guidance on this from the Church or from Nyerere, for that matter. I think it would be safe to say that both wanted to avoid another conflict so that would be my aim also. The problem was how to do it without alienating one side or the other or both.

True to his word, Joseph had arranged a meeting so I was soon sharing sundowners on Nkomo's porch. "Call me Joshua," he said, "I don't like too much formality and you won't get anywhere here in Africa if you try it. You Catholics have become marginalised in today's society because you ignored the issues of land for too long, and then sat on the fence over our struggle for independence so what are you here for?"

I must admit that this opening statement took me by surprise and I had to think fast. I had not expected the Church to come into our discussions in any way so I sidestepped the issue, falling back on Joseph's advice. "Thank you for seeing me, sir," I began, "the Holy Father wishes you well and only wants to help in your ambitions for land reform and eventual independence."

Now this was my first mistake and he picked up on it straightaway with a menacing growl. "Why is he suddenly taking such an interest and what does he mean by eventual?" Nkomo asked. "Is that to be this year, next year sometime or never?" He smiled at his own little joke and said, "No. Don't answer, let's just go in and have a nice cup of tea."

Tea helps, doesn't it, and I began to feel a little more relaxed as he broadened the conversation into somewhat less contentious areas such as his garden of which he was quite proud. Eventually though, I had to return to my mission and I suddenly had a brainwave. "Tell me, Joshua," I said following his informal manner, "Tell me, what is it that you would like me to do?"

Now I was in the ascendency as he was taken off guard and there were just a few uncomfortable moments before he spoke. "That is a very generous offer," he said, "and I have two options for you. The first is to go home and stop meddling in our affairs. Your past record is not good in that respect. My second is one where you can really be of help, to us, to your church and also to the Kariba leper colony where I would like you to go." Now he was miles ahead of me. In no way had I considered this a possibility, having had dreams of playing an important central role in the inevitable conflict to come. Once more, my pride had let me down as I realised that this was yet another important lesson in life for me to learn. It follows that I had to accept his second proposition humbly and even gratefully although, I don't think that this assignment was at all what the Holy Father had in mind for me, or was it? *He moves in mysterious ways,* they say and don't I know it.

Within a week, I was in Kariba where I took up a simple role of 'helper' under the watchful eye of Sister Alice. She exuded love and compassion and I felt a renewal in my bones as I worked alongside her. However, I could not be unaware that Kariba is the location of one of the most important river dams in Africa and adjacent to the world-famous Victoria Falls. The spray in the breeze could be sensed at all times and, of course, at dawn the many birds of the region came for an early shower while all I had was a basin. "It's the dawn birds," I could hear myself saying, "I love you, Elda."

Sister Alice could not quite hear what I said and remarked, "You seem happy today, Luke," and I was, with my memories and my newfound focus in life. However, the colony was not entirely cut-off from the outside world because supplies of one sort or another had to be delivered and vehicles passed by from time to time. I hope that I did not ignore my duties for the sick but these two factors intrigued me. Firstly, within the deliveries for food and hygiene equipment, I spotted a Russian name on a large box. It said *Kalashnikov* and I knew what that meant. Then I observed that most of the trucks were petrol tankers of one sort or another, some were old, converted farm trucks and others in the full livery of Agip and even Aeroflot down here on the ground.

There was little doubt that Kariba was in the frontline for the anticipated conflict to come, lepers or no lepers, but now I had another dilemma and it all came down to choices again. Was I to be a spy or a priest or both?

After some weeks of consideration, I decided to relate my concerns to Nkomo himself via a 'diplomatic bag' service that operated from the Colony. I had to wait some considerable time for a reply but in the meantime, I established very warm and cordial relationships with some of the leper community. It's easy to say but 'they' were just like us. Just like me as well if I'd been African. Disfigurements aside, they had personality and skills as in any other group. A favourite family of mine were the Mutasas, a mum and a dad and three lovely children, who had known no other than this restricted life. I spoke to Miriam one day and asked her what life was like. "It is wonderful," she said, "every day is as God has made it to be and we are grateful for his mercies and for Sister Alice, of course." Once more, I felt humbled and determined to stay longer if that is what my future held but naturally it wasn't. I finally received a reply from Nkomo asking me to transfer lock stock and barrel to an important trade union camp just outside Salisbury. His letter thanked me for my work but added that now he had something very important to show me and it was *top security*. I said farewell to my new friends and set off once again. Where was HE leading me to this time, I wondered.

The trade union HQ was set out rather like a military camp but I ignored this implication for now. Nkomo greeted me with genuine bonhomie and as usual invited me in for tea. It struck me that tea was the lifeblood of the community in a true social sense here, whereas in Kenya, it had been an economic one. Formalities over, he began, "Now you don't have to sign the Official Secrets Act," he said, "because we haven't got one. That's the present government's prerogative for the time being, but I would like you to assure me that you will not reveal anything of that which I tell you or show you today."

I affirmed that he could rely on me and crossed myself. "Hope to die," I said and smiled.

He just grunted and said, "Well, we hope that won't be necessary, don't we? Follow me please." He now led me into an inner chamber that reminded me very much of those Battle of Britain chartrooms that I had seen on film, with the maps laid out, staff with pointers and a group of officers and onlookers up in the gallery. It was just like that except we were the only two in the room. "Let me present *Operation Freedom*," he said, "now look at the map and what do you see? Can you see Kariba, for example?" I looked very closely and nodded. "Now, can you now see a red line going from Kariba to the North?" he continued and once more I said yes so his next question went into more detail. "You will have seen that Kariba is just on the Rhodesian/Zambian border with Lusaka, the Zambian capital a few miles further on and beyond that is the world-famous Copper Belt including the towns of Ndola and Kitwe. But look further. Where is the red line going now?"

I peered as it was barely dawn but I could make out the towns he had highlighted and I read them out to him. "Well, firstly there is Tunduma, then Mbeya and next is Iringa then Morogoro and lastly Dar es Salaam," I said triumphantly.

"Well done," said Nkomo, "so which countries are involved on that route then?"

This felt a bit like an oral exam but I knew the answer to that one. "Well, it must be Zambia and Tanzania," I said, wondering how this geography lesson had anything to do with Rhodesia.

Joshua saw that I was puzzled so he simply said, "Let's have a cup of tea and I'll complete the picture for you."

I enjoyed the tea and looked out of the window in the larger lounge to which he had directed me. I knew that this was an important moment, and I wished that Elda had been there to advise me, and suddenly there she was, now as a lovely parakeet settling on the veranda. "Hi, Elda." I said.

"I'm taking you into my confidence for three reasons," said Nkomo. "The first is that you have seen some of our preparations, the second is that you know Tanzania and the third that you are an expert in website accounts and we need those skills." I was agreeably surprised that my mini course way back at the university now gave me such a reputation. "You, my dear Luke, are one of the very few people who know about *Operation Freedom* which is the essential planning necessary for us, if and when Smith declares UDI. In this scenario, the British will be our allies but they are unlikely to commit forces, although they may help in other ways. Our job will be to make life uncomfortable for the Rhodesian forces, who are a combination of regulars, territorials and police. However, they also have a small but formidable air force of Vampires, Hunters and Canberra bombers and we have none.

"This is the military side of things but the economic side is important too, especially with regard to the Zambian copper that has become a staple item in world trade. We suspect that one of Smith's first actions will be to cut off the copper belt from supplies of oil, so an alternative will have to be found and that is where our 'red route' comes in. It is nothing less than a plan for fuel landed at Dar to make its way by road to Ndola and Kitwe. It is 1000 miles and the majority of the route is 'murram' track with very little tarmac. Costs could be high so we must try to make it all an inviting proposition for international investors. The road is vital, for without it the Zambian economy will collapse and the London Stock Exchange will go into free-fall. So where do you come in, you might ask?" He paused and looked at me closely waiting for a response but I *held my fire* to hear what else he had to say so he continued, "Well, your experience lies in Dar so that is where we want you to go. Firstly, to create a very close liaison with the PFB (the Petroleum Finance Board) so that carriage and finance arrangements will be secure, and secondly, in order to find entrepreneurs with trucks of all shapes and sizes who are out to make a quick buck, no questions asked. We must be ready, Luke, because a storm is surely on its way. You asked me what you might do and I have given you my answer. I just hope that the Pope will think that this counts as a 'mission'." Here he sat back and waited.

I must admit that I was doubtful about the whole thing but I decided to accept for a number of reasons, one that I would be back on familiar territory, two that I believed it might curtail the imminent war a bit, and three that I might get to see my 'family' in Naivasha again, to kiss my little Lou and to hug my lovely Elda.

Later that day, we went into some details. I was told that I would operate as *Tanga transport* which would allow me some anonymity in a world where suspicion would be rife. My base would be a partly abandoned Sisal farm at Mziba, just outside Dar. There would be plenty of space for fuelling and maintenance of such trucks as TT dealt with, but much of the carriage would be done by subcontractors with my office dealing with the paperwork, contracts and insurance. Nkomo said that they expected at least 100 of the former and as many, again for the latter and we would not be the only show in town. I had seen the Agip and Aeroflot emblems at Kariba but there were many more including Total and Sara from Yugoslavia. I was also given a supervisory role that included trips along the route in a spotter plane, or breakdown pickup truck on this 'Hell Run' to keep our drivers safe. We were to have two main partners operating from the farm, the first was Kristos Almiros who owned the farm itself and the second was the main Mercedes Benz dealer, a Major Kent from Nairobi. Almiros would provide 10 Fiat trucks, but Kent planned at least 50, including 25x 2620s and 25x 1618s. Nkomo said that we should thus be able to compensate for the lost fuel due to UDI sanctions.

"Good luck," he said as he waved goodbye. My reply would have been unprintable. To be honest, I did not think that I was up to the job, and not even sure what 'the job' was except to support the diverse anti-government forces that were now assembling. It was not just the prospect of UDI that had spooked Nkomo but, very personally, the killing of eleven of his followers in Bulawayo itself following a spate of riots. This, in turn, had led to more repressive government action and, in turn, to more riots. He decided to meet up with Nyerere and Kaunda, the PM of Zambia, to see if they might agree to a common approach but there were so many variables. Nkomo told me that Kaunda blew hot and cold, asserting 'nonviolence' whilst affirming that 'blood would have to be spilled'.

All this was above my head, of course, as I began to bring my small 'forces' into shape in one way or the other, but as I have said, we were a very diverse bunch. To be honest, I liked Kristos very much. He seemed to be an accomplished businessman man and a bit of a conman as well, a double dealer with personality, the kind that you just cannot refuse, and it was his wily approach that led to favourable PFB contracts for us. Above all though, he was a family man and the farm was his home. He was always surrounded by his children and grandchildren and those of others as he walked around the barns 'supervising' the feverish activity that was usually taking place on the impressive trucks that had begun to assemble there. He acted as if this was 'his' world but the truth was that it wasn't at all, because Mercedes had assigned three engineers from Stuttgart to this enterprise and they protected their charges like Tiger Tanks and kept aloof. I was in the middle, of course. I needed both but it was not easy to keep the peace as priorities and personalities sometimes flared. However, I was very lucky to have an ally in the shape of Kristos' wife, Miriam (I say 'shape' advisedly, as she was a rather buxom lady). I suspect that this farm and others run by a thriving Greek community of Sisal farmers had always been the centres of social activity, and it was still the same. Nearly every day was a day to celebrate something as food was served and dancers whirled around the dusty barns. They knew how to have fun and I got more than my fair share of kisses. I thought of Elda at such times and wished that she might share these moments of joy. At such a moment, I realised that I might only have a few months before an actual declaration of UDI, so I asked for permission to go to Naivasha and I was soon on my way. I'd like to say on my way 'home', but it wasn't quite like that, although Kristos and Miriam had shown me what a happy family life could be like.

So, up to the gates with Elda standing on the porch holding a small bundle and I felt wonderful. She embraced me, handed me the bundle and said, "Luke, this is Michael. Michael, this is your Uncle Luke." I was taken aback but realised at once that I'd been away for more than a year, and then I noticed that on the steps beside her was a pram with the sound of a happy child chortling.

"Elda, my dear Elda," I said, "we are all so lucky, aren't we? Can I hold Lou-Lou now, please?"

Gordon was away, she said so we had a meal and went to bed but as dawn broke, I heard a tap on my door. "Come and see," she said, "it's the dawn birds again." We sat on the veranda holding hands and then she turned to me and simply said "Gordon has gone," and started to cry.

I held her tight with reassuring words as tears ran down my face as well. "Don't worry," I said, "he'll be back, I'm sure." But I didn't know the half of it.

Part Four
Elda's Last Word

Foreword

It has been left to me to complete our story. You will have read how the three of us met at the University in Birmingham and how we all ended up in Africa. Friendship is an elusive thing and I think that we have remained friends throughout, despite split loyalties on occasions. However, personalities come into it also, and people do not always behave in the way they intended to, and outcomes are not always how we might have wished them to be. However, I believe that love is a longer-lasting sentiment and I think that we have all shared this at different times as well. You have seen how friendship, love and loyalty have influenced our story for better or worse on our journey, so now I'll tell you the rest.

Chapter One
Love and Loyalty

I had been very pleased to see Luke after such a long time but my last few months with Gordon had been sheer torture for us both. Agreed, we had the new baby to distract us, but as his National Service was shortly coming to an end, there was our future to consider, and it was on this that we disagreed strongly. Neither of us wanted to return to the UK so we began to look for options in Africa. I opted for a continued life in Kenya or even Tanzania, but Gordon had his heart set on Rhodesia. He had met many Afrikaans auxiliaries during his military service and most of them had gone south to Rhodesia and 'a better life', they had said. I must admit that I had reservations about the prospect and told him so.

"Don't you think there's going to be trouble there?" I asked him.

"Maybe there will be some but let's ask our friends and neighbours here what they think." This was a crafty move from Gordon because we both knew what our neighbours thought, most of whom were Afrikaans stock as well. We held an informal party and many well-wishers attended as if we had gone already and Tak van der Vaak made a speech.

"Dear friends," he said, "the future lies in Rhodesia. The Prime Minister is Sir Edgar Whitehead and he's got his head screwed on. He wants to bring the Bantu and the Boers together and he has proposed to change the Land Apportionment Acts in favour of the natives. Land for peace, you might say." With that he sat down to much applause but his words had made me even more uneasy. Bantu, Boer and Native were hardly the language of compromise, it seemed to me but I decided to support Gordon, if only for a short while. Later, as we lay on our bed, I told him what I had decided and he was over the moon.

"Let's try six months or a bit more," I said, "maybe Mrs Botha will take the children in her kindergarten for a short period and we can send for them later." Over the next few months, we made plans despite the changes that we heard about in Rhodesia. Apparently Whitehead had been defeated by a new party called the Rhodesia Front headed by the fairly insignificant Winston Field. This was bad enough, but within months, he was replaced by Ian Smith with a much more ambitious agenda with propaganda to match such as 'The white man is master', 'We must defend civilisation' and 'Blacks will never rule here'.

I sensed a disaster and told Gordon that I thought that we should defer our plan for now. Unfortunately it seemed that he did not want to lose face amongst our neighbours and simply said, "Well, are we going or not?"

I hesitated, playing for time I suppose as I remembered the Mau Mau terror in Kenya, then I had a brainwave. "Let's give it the weekend and think it over," I said, "I know, let's go to Lake Victoria for a break." I sidled up to him and gave him my most inviting smile until his resistance gave in.

"All right," he said, "we'll go but I hope you know what you're letting yourself in." I sure did because, although the first idea about moving filled me with anxiety, the second about Angus and his sporran filled me with excitement.

Lake Victoria, or more properly Lake Mwanza, is bordered by Kenya, Uganda and Tanzania and is famous for its Nile perch, but I had another form of fishing on my mind. We took the ferry the *Bukoba* from our Kenyan side across the lake to Entebbe which is in Uganda and there we found the charming *Two Friends* beach house. The building was a mixture of straw and thatch combined with the normal brick/plaster of a normal hotel and our room overlooked the lake. Within sight were the Ssese Islands with their proliferation of bird life, 'fishermen' like me. The few days drifted by in a haze of love and emotions that we had not found for months and then one day Gordon turned to me and said, "You know that I love you, my dear Elda. I'm so glad I have you and I couldn't possibly live without you," with which he held me so tight I could hardly breathe.

I hugged him tight and hoped that it would last forever but soon we were back at Naivasha stretched out on our veranda, and I was so happy. Just to prove it, I turned to him and said, "I love you, my own sweet Angus. Never doubt it." Then I settled back with a smile, hoping for a loving response but when it came, it took me by surprise.

"Well, are we going then?" he said.

I was shell shocked and deeply hurt and ran from the room crying. He had totally ruined our lovely romantic weekend and my world had fallen apart. The words of Oscar Wilde came into my thoughts as he had said, *The brave man does it with a knife*, but he had not said how much it hurt. I know that

I slept for hours because it was dawn when I awoke to the sound of our B52 pelicans on the lake outside our window. I turned to touch Gordon but he was not there so I got up and made for the kitchen to make tea and there beside the kettle was a small note.

I love you, Elda, it said, *Don't worry. I'll send for you soon.*

This was all very well for him, I thought. I felt like a jilted bride and refused to get up again for days but soon a sense of pragmatism took hold. I would go when/if he asked and we could start again, couldn't we?

Then another bombshell struck my little world as the anticipated UDI was declared, despite the threatened sanctions on coffee and oil. Smith immediately isolated Gibbs the Governor, and both sides began preparations for a very long struggle. Nearly all the Christian churches including the Catholics, supported Gibbs but it did him no good.

I remember thinking at the time that Luke would agree with that, and then lo and behold, there he was on my doorstep. I realised that he and I were on the same social and political wavelength, but I loved Gordon and did not want to seem disloyal. He had sent me a few letters from Umtali Barracks where he was serving with the Rhodesian Defence Forces so after Luke left, I decided to travel south to renew that love that Gordon and I had only recently rediscovered.

Chapter Two
Love and Tragedy

As I arrived at Umtali barracks, Gordon was there to greet me and immediately smothered me with kisses. He then paraded me around in the officer's quarters like a prize racehorse. "Here she is," he exclaimed, "this is my lovely wife, Elda. Isn't she a gorgeous filly?"

I'm not sure that I liked this analogy but I sure liked the attention. He had very attractive and spacious married quarters and that first evening he took me, sat me down on a comfy settee with a glass of wine. "I want you to know how much I love you," he said, "And how grateful I am that you have come to be with me. I am aware that you had reservations but now I'd like to put your mind at rest."

This sounded like a good start so I snuggled up and just said, "I love you too and it'll be great when we are able to bring our family here, won't it?" He nodded and continued to tell me about the role of the Rhodesian Army in Umtali, stressing that it was really a 'border security' operation to assist in the supplies of fuel from Portuguese Beira to Rhodesia to elude the British sanctions.

"A group of Rhodesian terrorists called 'The Crocodiles' have been active here," he said, "and three years ago in 1964, they murdered a local farmer called Oberhauzer. They were captured and sentenced to be hanged but this caused such an international furore that it had been delayed. Most of us would just like to get it over with because the delay has led to more riots and more fruitless talking, most recently by PM Wilson and Smith aboard HMS Tiger on the high seas between Gibraltar and Morocco. It makes me smile to think of Wilson being seasick. There is also an Umtali Bishop named Abel Muzerewra who is seeking a 'third way', but I don't give him much of a hope with Nkomo and Mugabe almost literally calling the shots, and that's without mentioning Kaunda or Nyerere."

I was not at all comforted by Gordon's views on the subject but decided to keep quiet while he was being so attentive. "That's enough of all that," I said, "I've come a long way so let's go to bed now and you can show me your sporran again."

The next morning, he sprung a pleasant surprise namely that he had a weekend pass to visit the ancient port of Beira just across the border. "It'll be fun," he said, "as you know, the Portuguese have two colonies, Angola in the East and this one, Mozambique in the West. It's not easy for them because there is a 'terrorist' group called Frelimo that has to be taken into account as well as border raiders from our side, so security is vital."

All of this disturbed me even more but I was looking forward to some quiet moments with Gordon so I just agreed that we should go. The route from Umtali follows the 'Beira corridor' which is a main gateway to the hinterlands of Zambia and Rhodesia and it only took an hour. We were met by a young Portuguese girl from the tourist office and she showed us around for the next few days. Her name was Magda Rivera and she seemed to know everything one might need to know about the city from its foundation by the Portuguese as 'Beira' (previously Chiveve) in 1900. We stayed at the Grande Hotel, a Mecca for white Rhodesians in whose company Gordon felt quite at home and I liked to see him happy, but I was most contented at the Praia do Estoril, a lovely beach pavilion with views over the Indian Ocean. Naturally, seagulls were present in their hundreds and their very presence comforted me but Gordon didn't like them if they got too close.

Fortunately, he and I had plenty of time on our own and at such times I wished that we could be together more often, just in case. The fact is that the conflict had widened considerably from a military one to an economic one and this one was equally vicious. British sanctions after UDI had hardened attitudes on both sides especially where British interests were vulnerable, namely in oil, copper and coal. The copper belt was vital but so were the Wankie coalmines that were important in local terms, but also to supply Katanga.

After our lovely and loving weekend, it was back to business as usual for Gordon with his duties for the Army. He had reassured me on a number of occasions that his involvement was a local one, protecting the Beira corridor and that he could be home nearly every night. This suited me although the days could be lonely, and it was then that I met another army wife called Rosalind van Rose. I thought it was a lovely name and told her so and we soon became friends. Her husband, Max, was from Cape Town, one might say a displaced Boer, but they were happy in Rhodesia with a farmstead at Gwelo and planning to have a family very soon.

"He believes in apartheid and all that supremacy stuff," she confided in me one day, "but I'm a different kind of Christian, one who believes that all men (and women) are created equal." I told her that I felt the same and our friendship flourished.

So the next few months rolled by until one day as Ros and I were having tea, Gordon came home and told us some very disturbing news. "I've got orders to go to Wankie with my troop and Max will be going with me," he said, "We are leaving tomorrow with provisions for at least a month." Ros and I looked at one another in disbelief and I felt like asking if they could find someone else. I had that nasty feeling in my stomach that this would be no ordinary mission, and it wasn't just a feeling because Gordon had told me that more than one hundred terrorists had infiltrated the Zambezi valley, some 75 miles from Victoria Falls, headed for the coal mines at Wankie just a few weeks ago and the Army must stop them.

We barely had time to say our goodbyes before they were both off with a wave. "Goodbye, Dolly!" shouted Max as their truck pulled away. My mind went back to those tragic killing days on the Western Front during World War One that my father had spoken of. No time for that though as I could see that Ros was crying her eyes out.

The next few weeks were unbearable for us as we gleaned more information from the brigade HQ. A report said that our troops had been ambushed and pinned down for a substantial period and had been forced into hand-to-hand combat but air strikes had brought the situation under control. This sounded encouraging until I had a visit from Major General Starkie and I knew that it was bad news. I clung to Ros as we both waited for the worst. "I am sorry to tell you that Lt Bird and Sgt van

Rose were killed on active service this week," he said. "Please accept my heartfelt condolences."

Ros and I were lost for words and lost in our minds for the next few days and weeks and months and no amount of comforting words would help. 'I know just how you feel' is meant well, but no one does know as darkness falls with no sign of light or life. All I can say is that at least Ros and I had each other as we both faced our futures. There were funerals of course, beautifully arranged by the Army with all the trimmings and money wasn't a particular problem either as Army pensions were generous. No, the problems came with decisions about family and property.

For me, I thought it best to return to our house in Naivasha that was lease hold (so time limited) but mainly to see the children and have their dad buried by the lake. After that, I was not sure where I would go but I had a year (courtesy of the Army) to sort it out.

Ros had the same benefits but she was worried about the freehold title to her house in Gwelo that had been arranged by an agent on behalf of the Army. "It's not clear," she said, "In fact there are many appendices in a sort of code that I don't understand at all. I was very fortunate that Max dealt with all that. Many recruits in the Army had the same contracts and there was a clause that said we could only sell to persons agreed to by our agents. I told Max about my worries but he said, 'No problem, leave it to me, my darling' so I backed off."

I started to feel a sense of *déjà vu* as memories of the Anderson file came flooding back so, just on a hunch, I asked her for the name of the agent and she replied, "It's TLT or The Land Trust. I've been told that their property portfolio increases year by year and it's all in white Europeans' hands by virtue of the conditions imposed. Max told me that TLT were part of a much larger consortium known as TILT, in other words 'The International Land Trust'. They operate in many countries across the world with political as well as commercial clout for members and investors but all I wanted was a home for me and my children."

Here, she started to cry again and I sat next to her holding her hand, but quietly weeping as well. I also felt a certain empathy with her as she had decided to show her love for Max by supporting him against her own better judgement. Yes, I had 'been there' as well, and Luke's comments way back from college came to mind. It was all about choices, he had said, but that was the difficult bit.

Now we both had to attend to our immediate futures so I went back to Naivasha to lay Gordon to rest. Then I brought the children back with me to Umtali. I had the Army's permission to stay for a year so I had some breathing space to think about my future and to renew my friendship with Ros.

Chapter Three
Love and Destiny

I had barely unpacked my bags back in Umtali when I heard a soft tap on the door. I shivered because the last knock had been that which had informed me of the tragedy at the Wankie coal mine where Gordon and Max had been killed. I, therefore, hesitated before cautiously opening it to see Luke standing there with a small bunch of violets. I didn't know whether to laugh or cry so I did both and hugged him tight.

Lost and found in Birdland

Foreword

It is said that once trust is lost, it can never be found, but that doesn't account for the power of love. This book is somewhat of a sequel to my own novel *The Dawn Birds* as we left Luke and Elda on the brink of wedded bliss. Their farm at Lake Naivasha is now threatened by Rose Plantations and Greenhouses despoiling the lake's ecology, and they have different perspectives as to how to deal with it. Meanwhile her friend Ros had stayed on at the farm and she and Elda have surprisingly found a deep attraction and an intimate friendship. Elda has taken part-time work with the KPU in Nairobi, hoping to lead to sustainable development for all, with room for fishermen and farmers alike. Luke tends to support Kenyatta's KANU party with interests selling roses world-wide. However, he has also begun to make the best use of Elda's absence by beginning an 'affair' with Ros herself with tragic consequences. He knows he has been at fault, but he can't persuade God to help and he can no longer wriggle his way out. Can he find the love that they had lost, and could there be another way to save their marriage and prove his love for Elda again; and how indeed might the lovely Rosie help?

Chapter One
Luke's Wriggle Room

There is always a room, or maybe just a physical or metaphorical space where a final negotiation between one or more persons is given leave to be discussed. One may be up against it for many reasons, so a wriggle room is a valuable space in which any ruse, truth or untruth, may have to be deployed to achieve a favourable outcome, and hopefully to avoid an embarrassing impasse. Let's just call it a 'storm in a teacup', Luke would say. He knew his wriggle rooms like the back of his hand and could usually negotiate his way out of a problematic situation and save face without too much difficulty but this time it could be very different. It had all begun so simply and over such a trivial matter, and might easily have been brushed aside, had he observed the first rule of social survival. In other words, 'If you are in a hole, stop digging'.

Elda was laying the table for high-tea on the following day when she paused with a worried frown. "Luke," she said, "I had decided to use that nice anniversary tea-set that Jim and Judy gave us as they don't visit us very often but there are only three cups instead of four. Do you know what happened to the other one, dearest?"

Luke knew very well what had happened, but the truth could not be told if he was to survive the next few moments with Elda! A plausible explanation had to be conjured up fast and he did not have much time to wriggle, no time at all. There were two options, namely to tell the truth and lay bare his imperfections, or to tell a lie just this once…again. He had to think fast so the latter course seemed the best for now so he said. "I think that Suzy, the exchange student/au pair, broke it some time ago, dear, and we haven't used it since, so I didn't mention it after she left."

Elda sighed. "I wish you had told me, Luke," she said, "I might have found another or bought a new set. Never mind, let's find the old one. Ros, can you come and help, please? You seem to know how to set a table. I don't know what I'd do without you but thankfully I don't have to. Men may have their uses but laying table isn't one of them. We can use the old tea set but put out the crystal glass."

As she said this, she smiled and gave Luke a peck on his cheek. "That's from St Elda and the dawn birds," she said, "Now please find the champagne and put it on ice." She had acquired this saintly soubriquet from growing up close to the saintly examples of St Hylda of Whitby Abbey and her birds and she hinted that as a Whitby herself, she could always call on them if she was in trouble. She hoped that this might keep Luke on his toes from time to time but it didn't seem to work.

Meanwhile Luke had mellowed on this occasion and responded with bird sounds, "Honk/Hoot/Beep/Beep," and they all laughed. "Can you recognise them?" he said.

She had met Ros in Zimbabwe and brought her home after they both lost their husbands fighting for Smith's UDI some years ago. She had soon settled in as 'Auntie Ros' to Lou-Lou and Michael and had seen them grow into young adults and they had grown fond of her and despite their different backgrounds, Elda had found a kindred spirit. Luke had grown 'perhaps a little too fond' of her as well so, with Elda away for the weekend and no rehearsal, a series of fleeting fumbles on the settee sent the crockery flying. So that's what happened to the cup after all! Ros and he would have to be much more careful in the future, 'if there was to be a future', he mused. Then he started to panic as he thought of the consequences that might entail from another slip like that, so perhaps now would be a good time to 'finish' his steamy but casual affair with Ros. He knew that she didn't care too much about him but that she liked the attention, but the thought of coming clean with her and even more so with Elda scared him to bits, not to mention God and his eternal damnation.

More to the point, would Elda remember that they had actually used the full tea-set after Suzy left and what then? He bit his fingernails, praying for a miracle.

So now he was damned if he confessed and damned if he didn't and he felt as if he was running out of 'wriggle room'. As he tossed and turned that night, he dreamt that they were back at the university where they had first met, he a Roman Catholic Jesuit Priest and she an excitable student. There had been an immediate attraction between them, bedevilled by Church dogma as he tried to 'be good'. Yes, he kept his physical distance but he could not rely on his dreams to behave, and sometimes there was tell-tale evidence in the morning, 'sins' that would literally have to be washed away before sheets went to the laundry.

St Augustine had said, "Lord, make me good but not yet." and this axiom suited Luke very well. However, St Paul's

Epistle to the Romans was less forgiving. "I see another law in my members, warring against the law of my mind and bringing me into captivity to the law of sin, which is in my members."

Could it be that St Paul was equating all sex with sin, he wondered and…"couldn't we come to a compromise, dear God?" he pleaded before he was able to drop off to sleep, hoping to find a less prescriptive Elda there, but in this, he was disappointed as well.

"So, you are the famous Father Luke," she said in the dream, "I'm Elda Whitby. I fancy you like mad but you must change your habits to get me." They both laughed at this double entendre as she told him more about St Hylda and the dawn birds. She also confided that she was a guardian gatekeeper of the 'Sea Bird Society' as they challenged the deeds of land ownership in today's society. "It'll get me into trouble one day," she had said, "but I know that I can trust you because I love you."

Luke was wide awake now but sweating profusely as her words rang in his ears. So love was trust and vice versa after all and this did not suit him one bit as it did not allow for his prevarication on matters romantic. He knew that he had failed Elda in the past and he had regretted it ever since despite his many attempts to atone over the years. Now the question of trust had come up again and the dream only highlighted his dilemma. If he had been 'allowed' three loves, they would have been Elda, Ros and God, but in what order?

Fortunately, he felt that he did not have to choose this time over the teacup because long ago, he had decided not to rank them at all, but that he would just 'have his cake and eat it', re-interpreting the Bible to 'Render unto Caesar' for his own purposes. Elda would have her marriage, Ros would get her playtime and God must be patient. The trouble with this scenario was that the others had not agreed to it and anyway each had their own priorities that he must accommodate to if he might 'eat his cake' in peace.

No chance of that, Luke, as the three of them sat down for breakfast on the veranda. This was always Elda's favourite time of day as she surveyed the lake looking for any unusual activity. "They're a bit sleepy today," she observed, "Oh, there's a few now. Good morning, my lovelies, Mummy's here."

Ros smiled but Luke was rather irritated. "You call them as if they are human," he said, "Why don't you hoot and honk like they do?" This might have been funny but Elda understood Luke too well and knew that it was a put-down. Why? Well, she never quite knew why with him but maybe it was all about the cup, but that begged another question as to why he would wish to be so secretive. Was he hiding something else altogether?

Anyway, now she decided to make light of it by making noises. "Hoot, Honk and Beep Beep for the geese," she called out. This eased the tension as Ros and Luke burst into laughter with their own Honks and Beeps and Hoots. Then Oteo, the house boy, brought breakfast of salmon steaks, 'Caught this morning, Bwana' with grapefruit and tea.

They got their newspapers a few days late at *Haven Farm*. This had been Elda's idea for a name when she had bought the property with her first husband, Gordon, before he was killed in action in Zimbabwe (more on him later). When they had been searching for something suitable, they found out that the farm next-door belonged to Joan and Alan Root, well known then for their filming but later as environmental activists, so *Haven Farm* seemed most appropriate, although they did not intend to keep hippos or a large menagerie.

Now Elda opened the paper and after a few moments, she let out an agonised cry. "It's JM," she said, "He's been assassinated. Shot and dumped on an Ant Hill near Nairobi. It's so terrible."

You would have thought that Luke would sympathise but it wasn't his style. He was more of a prankster or a 'joke' man and was yet to grasp that this was serious. "JM dead?" he said, "So what happens to Peter Pan then?" There followed an awkward silence as Elda left the room crying, followed by Ros who gave him a scathing look as she wrapped a comforting arm around a trembling Elda.

"You men will never understand feelings," she said, "can't you see that she is upset? Don't bother to follow us. We don't need you." Luke thought that this was a bit strong but just shrugged his shoulders and began to read.

JM ASSASINATED TODAY – 8 JUNE 1975, IS A DAY OF INFAMY. KENYA'S BRIGHT LIGHT JM KARIUKI IS DEAD.

The story went on to explain that J M Kariuki, one of Kenyatta's early followers, had been shot and left on an anthill as a visible sign of disrespect. There was more detail and conjecture about who and why, but now Luke felt sick and didn't know how to make it up to Elda. One thing was for sure, he would need all the wriggle room he could muster but even that might not be enough. He thought of saying a prayer but felt that God had ceased to listen to him. The point was that, in her duties in Nairobi, she had met JM a number of times and liked him very much. Luke knew that JM was working with the environmentalists at the lake to seek out ways of sustainable development in which the Roots were also involved and in which Elda was involved.

Could it get worse? Oh yes, it could because, unknown to Elda, Luke had accepted an advisory commission to a major horticultural company 'Astracon' who were developing innovative ways of growing roses at the lakeside. Rose production was in its infancy but later it was to become a major exporter for the country but with unforetold consequences as the lake levels eroded.

Luke was on the horns of a dilemma again. His wriggle room was vanishing fast because he knew that this would be a major sin on his 'charge' sheet from Elda but the chances of keeping it secret were minimal. If she did find out as before in the UK, it would be the cover-up that would upset her. "I trusted you, Luke," he could hear her saying. So why not tell the truth and get it over with now? There were two factors that made this difficult for him. Firstly, his self-esteem, call it pride if you will, as his opinions were valued and he had opportunities to meet the rich and famous with who-knows-what influence later on. He simply could not lose face. The second difficulty was financial. This was a well-paid job and they needed the money for the farm and the children's schools. *I know,* he thought, *I'll ask God,* but when he did there was a silence again.

The next day with the tea party over, it was time for bed and hopefully a quiet night. They lay side-by-side until he turned to her and said, "I'm so sorry, my darling. I wouldn't upset you for the world but I'm rather clumsy sometimes. You know how much I love you."

She smiled and turned to him, "Show me how much then." she said and threw back the covers. He was a rascal she knew that but she loved him just the same.

The night was sultry and their love was gentle and, in the morning, they were woken by the dawn birds on the lake once more. "I know," she said, "let's take a boat out to see what damage those rose growers are doing. I haven't seen a hippo for ages. Let's go and see. It's such a lovely day."

Luke paused before replying. He was running out of wriggle room again and did not want a confrontation with Elda on the lake. "Not today, dear," he said, "I've got a funny tummy. It must have been the salmon." But as he said this, he realised that toxic fish were part of the problem for Elda, so he just said, "I wouldn't want to meet up with a horny hippo looking for his mate." Elda giggled. He could always make her laugh.

"Another day then." she replied with a smile.

Chapter Two
Elda and a Storm in Teacup

Although they had known each other for many years, Elda had to confess that Luke had played havoc with her emotions on many occasions and continued to do so now. With hindsight, she had to admit that much of this was not his fault as her hormones ruled her head from time to time. At college, she had followed him around like a lovesick puppy but later, when they met up by chance at Barnham Railway Station, she felt like a bitch on heat and it seemed only moments before he had whisked her off for a romantic break at Selsey Bill with seabirds squalling outside their room. From there to a magical romance seemed a certainty until she found that she had lost trust in him and for her, trust and love were indivisible. "A storm in a teacup," he had said when she pointed out her disappointment over a matter of land acquisition. "You got what you wanted so why did it matter how?"

She had looked at him with pity and contempt. "It's over for good, Luke," she said, "I can't love someone I don't trust."

Years had passed by and now they were living as a married couple on Lake Naivasha, so we ought to briefly take a peek at how that came about.

Soon after the Luke affair, Elda met up with another university colleague, Gordon Bird, just before he had to do his National Service. This took him to Kenya and, although not married, Elda went as well with the Queen Alexander Nursing Corps. Unfortunately, her interest in 'land reform' led to meetings with Kikuyu leaders and resulted in a 15-year gaol sentence that might only be mitigated if she was a married woman within Gordon's regiment. At this time, Luke was in Holy Orders in Kenya also and was able to organise and officiate at their wedding. This was a traumatic moment for them both, as the erstwhile lovers now stood on opposite sides of the altar, but Elda realised what a sacrifice he had made and was to recall it later.

Now matters took a most unfortunate turn with the declaration of UDI in Rhodesia. Gordon had finished National Service and joined the RDF (Rhodesian Defence Forces) and Elda went with him, "but only for six months," she insisted, as they intended to retain their farm at Naivasha for their growing family. On the other hand, Luke was appointed to a Papal Mission to 'nurture a love of Mother Church within the rebel force the ANC', by the Vatican. Distressed by this anomaly, Luke visited the farm from time to time being appointed godfather and 'Uncle' to the children, Lou-Lou and Michael. Then came a dreaded moment when Gordon was killed on active service at the Wankie Coal Mines. With such distress, Elda retreated to Naivasha bringing another Rhodesian widow with her for her recovery. This was Rosalind Rose and she soon became part of the family as 'Auntie' Ros and they were a deep comfort to each other in these dark days, often sharing tear-stained pillows at night until they were exhausted.

So then there were four of them unless you include part-time au pair, Suzy, until Luke arrived having resigned his mission for the Vatican in Rhodesia, soon-to-be Zimbabwe. "The Pope wants me to help Bishop Muzerewa," he justified himself to Elda, "But I had been sent to help Nkomo who is now in prison. His Holiness seems to think it's all a 'storm in a teacup' that will blow over and peace will break out soon. I tried to tell him how wrong he was and I was right." Soon after that, they were 5 because Luke proposed marriage and Elda accepted. She was an optimist and with the B52 pelicans circling around to encourage her, she had decided to trust him, and this brings us up to date.

***

Much had obviously taken place since that traumatic break-up so long ago, but now Elda decided that Luke was a reformed character with only a hint of being so self-centred as before. It was true to say that he had gone to extraordinary lengths to assuage his guilt over the 'land' affair, even to the point of helping her to marry Gordon, but unfortunately, there had been other signs of Luke's determination to make excuses or just to find his way out of a difficult situation by trying to reduce it to an irrelevance. 'A storm in a teacup', he would often say but why now, over a real teacup?

She had always kept just a little bit of scepticism in reserve when it was needed and hearing him explain the missing cup as yet another 'storm in a teacup' made her prick up her ears. *I've heard that one before*, she thought, but she concluded that it just was his way of avoiding confrontation, and she loved him so. "I call him the Artful Dodger," she explained to friends whilst keeping an open mind. As before, she was unable to recognise duplicity until it was too late so she was content to work away from home for the Odinga Party with J M Kariuki and the more socialist KPU in Nairobi.

She never worried about being away for periods of time, sometimes weeks, as she supported land reform and protested against the potential pollution of Lake Naivasha itself that many said was caused by the increased rose growing on the lake shore. Vested interests supported this kind of activity so it was necessary to find supporters to work against Kenyatta's and Kanu's growing power. In this, she was lucky to have become friends with Joan Root who owned the farm next door. Joan and her husband Alan were important filmmakers but, following their divorce, Joan had retreated to their Naivasha farm to find peace and serenity as well as abundant wildlife including the hippos. More recently, she had become very active in seeking sustainable lake development, and this led to threats from some rose companies and politicians. One late evening and before the JM assassination, she sat on Elda's veranda and confided her hopes and her fears as the sun went down.

"I am so glad that we met," she said, "It seems that we've both had our ups and downs, almost literally in my case when Alan and I were filming in a hot air balloon. But although we found 'Hippo Farm' together, we divorced soon after and I began to spend more time here, alone at first and then with a few friends from the lake management committee and I am so glad that you are now one of us. It's a pity that we haven't seen more of Luke but I suppose he is a busy man. We learnt a lot from the Bruntland Report and it seems to us that here

at 'our' lake as elsewhere there is a case for planned *sustainable development and not speculative farming on the perimeter. Reports say that the water levels are falling and pump technology from the rose farms draws in small fish leaving the predatory larger ones to starve. Some farmers insist that water for irrigation is in a sealed container and, therefore, not harmful but we don't accept that. However, we are hopeful that, if we might achieve a quorum of support around the lake itself, everyone will benefit in the long run. Unfortunately, investors such as Astracon often want to make a 'quick buck' and don't mind how they get it. I have not wanted to tell you this but my home has been raided on quite a few occasions, maybe just to scare me off and it is very frightening at night on my own, I can tell you. You are lucky to have a small household with you but I advise you all to have a 12-bore shotgun close by. Just be careful that's all."*

Elda was not entirely surprised but it was rather unnerving to say the least so, when in doubt bring the teapot out, she decided. "One lump or two?" she said.

It might be appropriate to mention here that Joan Root was murdered in her home a few years later and her killers and those of Kariuki have not yet been found.

Forewarned is indeed forearmed and she was determined to speak to Luke and Ros about guns and Astracon the next day but she was booked to go on a mission up country for the KDP. It was important, so the domestic arrangements would have to wait for a while. "Look after Ros and the farm," she said happily as she drove away, and unknown to her, Luke did just that.

Suzy, the au pair, had finished her contract so there was plenty of time for a kind of flirtatious friendship to bloom between Ros and Luke. He was too focussed on the chase to think much about Elda at all. "Just a bit of fun," he would assure himself but Ros did worry and said so.

"This is going nowhere," she said, "I'm extremely fond of Elda so let's cool off for a bit. I don't want to hurt her."

This suited Luke to an extent so he agreed and all might have been well if it had not been for a chance find (a lock of hair) by Elda as she looked through some financial papers one day. This might have changed everything if she had not previously decided that she would do anything to save her marriage, even if another case of mistrust had occurred. She thought that she owed that much to Luke, given his stoicism over her marriage to Gordon. The lock of hair that she actually had discovered was a lock of Rosalind's hair neatly entwined in an eternity ring that she had presented to Luke a year ago; and now it also dawned on her that the four teacups had been present after Suzy left. The find had happened by accident but what was she to do about it? It seemed to be a fatal breach of trust once again (with a Suzy cover-up for some unknown but suspicious reason as well), but now she was more cautious as to how to proceed. But this must surely be the last straw. Should she allow lack of trust to trump love, or would she give her love a trump hand to win the day? Two hearts maybe!

Her plan was to arrange a favourable situation in which Ros and Luke might both be satisfied with a decision she would take but without realising why; so the idea of a celebration party (with new tea-set) came to mind. But what would they celebrate, she wondered? Well, she already knew that she had the perfect answer. Ros would be offered a fulltime job in Nairobi courtesy of Odinga himself as Elda 'found she could not manage the increasing workload'. Elda knew that she and Ros shared a deep belief in socialist principles as well as a personal chemistry so there would be no interview and the job was presented as a fait accompli at the party.

She tapped the table and spoke, "We shall all miss you terribly, Ros, and we hope you will keep in touch." She really meant it but Luke looked bemused as if he had lost a cookie jar. "To celebrate, I have booked a weekend for two at Treetops as it is open again now. So let's all raise our glasses or teacups to a happy future for us all wherever we may be. Cheers!"

True to her word, she had arranged a Valentine's weekend at Treetops. It had been rebuilt following the Mau Mau attack and it retained much of its appeal. Their table was well adorned with roses, of course, but she had not really thought through this contradiction in her mind, hoping the matter of rose farming might not come up at all but she was to be disappointed. "Lovely, aren't they?" Luke said, "Lovely just like you. This was a lovely idea. Thank you, my precious," he said and held her hand.

She smiled appreciatively and replied, "Do you come here often?" and at this, they both laughed.

Soon afterward, they retired to a small sitting room for a nightcap when they were approached by a man she did not know. "Hello, Luke," he said, "So this is the lovely Elda you talk so much about. Don't forget next Tuesday. The MD is coming down especially to tie up that deal you worked on for

Astracon so I'll see you then." There followed a deafening silence before Elda started to cry. Then she got up and left the room without a word and then left the hotel in a taxi. Luke had a sense of *déjà vu*. Last time she had said that she would never trust him again; this time she said nothing but the palpable silence was much louder than before.

Was her vow to save her marriage 'regardless' to be broken? The next days would decide.

Chapter Three
The Ros Revelations

Elda had been quite correct in thinking that Ros would be over the moon with her new job in Nairobi and she barely gave a thought to a somewhat sulky Luke as the party wore on. To be honest, she was glad to be free of a difficult situation and she did care about Elda and the children. As she packed her bags over the next few days, she decided to write an apologia to Elda, setting out her sentiments since Rhodesia but also including the story about her life in Durban before marriage together with her hopes for the future. Here it is.

Dear Elda,

You know that I love you, but for me a consummated physical love is a difficult process. I was raped as a school girl in Durban and no one, but no one except my late husband has been my lover. That is not to say that I do not enjoy being admired and comforted in small ways by men that I like. Luke was one of them and I know that I should have deterred him but I got lonely at times. I am truly sorry that I broke your trust in me and I'm glad that we can all move on now. Actually my sexual inclination is towards women and probably always has been since Durban. Well, you know that from experience when I sidled into your bed that night when Luke was away and you were lonely too. Your touch was exquisite and I could not wait for more, rationalising that this form of bliss was no threat to Luke at all. Rather the opposite as you might have wanted to try new things with him.

I therefore settled on a need-to-know basis. Can you imagine what a bust-up there would have been with Luke if he found out for himself, and especially so if he had wider ambitions for me and him? Actually I do not think he had such intentions because it seems to me that he is somewhat addicted to danger and pleasure and he doesn't quite know where boundaries might lie. It's the world according to Luke which is his weakness as well as his strength. In my case, I was flattered and overwhelmed by his attention and I'm sorry.

You see, I had a wonderful childhood in Durban, the third largest city in South Africa with all modern amenities as well as a respectful attitude to the past. The Natal province is still called Kwa Zulu with many memorials to Shaka, even though it was the Dutch and British who created the modern city. Before and after the Boer Wars, the different nations vied for supremacy and the Voortrekkers left to travel north as far as Rhodesia where Bulawayo is now twinned with Durban. When Smith declared UDI, many of the old 'Dutch' South African families from Cape Town and other districts felt that they could create a new apartheid in the southern African autonomous region and my husband was one of them. I had to support him, of course, but my heart wasn't in it from the start and you know of the tragedy that ensued. He was a good man to me but he was a man with a man's attitude to women, namely me boss. This manifested itself in many ways not evident in public. Women were trophies on show or admired for generous causes but in the bedroom, it was all over in less than five minutes. This is what turned me on to lesbianism and I think that all women should give it a try so let's try it now. Settle comfortably on a chair or bed, sit back and close your eyes. Some soothing music might help. Now undo your blouse and circulate your hands around to feel your skin so lovely and soft. Now, tell me how you feel and let me hear your tones of pleasure, just ask me what you would like me to do. Now, put your hands down by your sides, close your eyes and say 'I love you'.

There, that wasn't too bad, was it? I suggest that trust is implicit here as you put your feelings in my hands and I would do likewise. It is a sad fact though that when desire becomes lust, then trust can be a casualty. So, let's get back to where we left off. It is late and you have gone to bed. It's a sultry night as you become aware that a figure is standing beside your bed. You smile. You can see that it is me even in the dusk and the last of the pelicans are settling down for the night.

"Can I join you?" I whisper seductively. You nod and fix your eyes on mine as my flimsy gown falls to the floor. You can just about see the shape of my arched and eager breasts. Now as I open my legs to climb in, there is a glimpse of a dark mound and a rich smell of perfume. "Kiss me, Elda," I say softly, "On my lips, yes."

Phew! So much for our second lesson and how are you feeling this time? Actually, I know just how you are feeling as I detected a small tremor from down there myself. So, who needs men, I say? I suppose that we all need a kind human touch, be it from male or female, but how that comes about is a matter of mutual negotiation with the deepest of respect in my opinion.

It is customary these days to arrange a prenup or a detailed wish and want list before embarking on a marriage, especially if it is a second or third one and maybe that should also be the case before a kiss is shared, lest misunderstandings lurk, as they normally do. Unfortunately, I suspect that most people are blown away by the hormonal impulse to mate as soon as possible, in other words to 'have sex'. Personally, I've given up worrying too much about 'dire consequences' and I suggest that you do the same. Be happy and above all, be sexy.

Love from Ros xx

Elda had felt very depressed after Treetops and the thought of a permanent break with Luke, but now she felt warm as she put the letter down. Then she awoke with a start and read it again as it dawned on her that once again, she had been judging Luke by her own standards and not by his. Ros seemed to see things much more clearly and was able to distinguish between love and lust and trust in a manner that Elda had not been able to in the past and even now. On a stroll around the lake on one occasion, Ros had reminded her that giving love is different to receiving love and both are different from sharing love.

"Confusion arises," she had said, "because these sentiments are not at all reciprocal, so I give you my love without regard for your love. It is complete in itself and it is mine to give and the reverse is true. Now I have observed, and you have told me that Luke has 'let you down', but that is because you have trained your love for him, to be dependent on his love for you. You must become free to love or not to love on your own terms and it is not a bartering game. You must accept that he loves you his way but loving him is different.

"By all means, cease to love him if he lets you down but please don't blame him for the loss of your love. He never said that he loved me and I did not expect him to. We enjoyed what we had and did not fret about what we did not have. I think you would be much happier if you could do that. You must grow to love with trust taken for granted and not hostage to mood swings or different definitions here and there. Love IS trust."

These words were her expression of what it means to love, and in them, Ros had sown the seeds of a way to go about finding it, giving it, receiving it and sharing it. We would say 'inadvertently' but perhaps there was a subliminal desire on her part to nurture a new affair.

Elda must have thought the same way but caution was her buzzword and now she set about practical ways to open up a space for a different kind of loving in her life. Firstly, she would make some small but important changes. For example, when she had set up the job for Ros in Nairobi, she had also organised a room for her at 122 Uhuru Street which happened to be the HQ of the KDP. It was a double-fronted Regency House with vast rooms, many let to students of which her children Louise and Michael were two. They had both taken up residence a few years back when they had begun their studies at Makerere University. So now the scene was set. Ros was given a vast attic room by the park, and Elda put her name down for the adjoining suite of rooms as an office but also as a bolthole.

She felt that she needed this space from Luke from time to time and, although he might not like it, she felt that he would accept it for their mutual benefit. However, and perhaps even more importantly, she would be sharing the house with Ros (and the KDP).

Chapter Four
Sanctuary

Elda had begun to realise that Luke's secrecy was not much to do with his love for her but just his way of protecting himself and, in a way, her as well. For example, if she had known about Luke and Ros, she would have been hurt but he still loved her and she him, so why make a fuss over a bit of hurt pride? Luke's involvement with Astracan was secretive, it's true, and money was a consideration, but he also knew about her commitment to property and ecological affairs so there could still be room for compromise. "I'm going to accentuate the positive from now on," she decided, "But will that mean a fundamental change of direction and even a change of identity within me? Has Ros set out a path that I haven't seen before and have I been paddling my canoe downstream instead of upstream?"

The answer was clear. She needed space for herself after years of being beholden to others. When she looked in her mirror, she questioned the image. "Who are you and more to the point, who am I?" The reply was unambiguous. "Why don't you find out then?"

This might be a rhetorical question but one that Elda now took seriously. The first step was to comprehend that she had not been a victim of love because she had always been a (more or less) willing accomplice with Luke and with Gordon, so 'finding herself' must mean just that and not necessarily the rejection of others. The second step was to acquaint Luke of her desire for a space to follow family, social, personal and political needs in Nairobi. "I'll be back often," she had said.

He seemed to accept this idea rather grudgingly given their recent impasse over Astracan but added (as one does), "I shall miss you terribly but who is going to feed the birds?" This is why she still loved him. He was able to elicit a smile even under difficult circumstances, but now she knew that it was part of his 'wriggle room' a ruse that gave him time to organise his thoughts and strategy to fit his purposes. She knew him so well but she didn't want to 'need' him so much. Going alone now was a big thing and she was not at all sure that she could cope. She tried to give herself a cogent reason as to what she would want her future to be like, and the answer was simply 'not the same', so she decided to keep a journal to check on her own progress as she set about a new life and here it is dated 4 July.

I arrived at 122 Uhuru Street this morning to be greeted by a small welcoming group with Ros obviously in charge, but there were also my kids Lou-Lou and Michael as well as a few smiling faces I did not know. I had not seen the children for a while so we all had a big hug before they took me up to my quarters with Ros leading the way. "We are on the ground floor," said Michael pointing to a small alcove, "Just through there we have separate rooms and there are four more but you've got some stairs to climb."

Now Lou-Lou chimed in with a laugh, "There's no lift but it's only four flights, the climb will do you good, Mum." I did my best to scowl at my lovely daughter but only managed a grin as we all set off carrying my paraphernalia.

With a huff and a puff, we arrived on a long landing going past a room marked *THE ROS ROOM* and Ros indicated it as we went by. "That's me," she said as we stopped, "and you are next door, just here."

Michael and Lou-Lou gave me a kiss and scurried off. "Got to go to lectures," he called over his shoulder, "See you for lunch." Then they were gone as Ros opened the door.

"Shall I carry you over?" she said with a smile.

"No, thanks," I replied, "I think I can manage it." I knew what she meant but I wasn't in a hurry. "Let's just step over the threshold together," and we did. Silly, isn't it? Such a small thing but I was drawing boundaries already and immediately regretting it. She had decorated the room neatly for me, although much of the furniture was cardboard boxes. The exception was the bed, a large elegant four-poster with clean linen and a sprinkling of lavender. "Oh, Ros," I said, "This is so lovely, shall we try it out?"

Now it was her turn to look quizzical. "Good idea," she said, "Which side do you want?"

"This side," I said as I flopped down with a bump and the most exquisite sound of 'Aaaah'.

Then the bed shook as Ros flopped down with an even louder 'Aaah' and I was rather glad that the children were not there. We just sat quietly now, maybe for half an hour or more before she got up. "I've got a letter to write," she said, "why don't you have a shower and freshen up? We'll go down to lunch in about an hour. Your shower and bath are just through there. Give me a knock."

It was teatime at the KPU-KAFF which, though sparse had all the ingredients for a 20th century Gunpowder Plot. "You can't be sure about anybody," said Ros, "for example, Jim Kito was KANU last week and now he's at the KPU table." She smiled at him and he smiled back.

Although Odinga was Vice President to Kenyatta at this time and they had been allies against the British, their views on a post-colonial Kenya were quite different.

'Jomo' Kenyatta KANU wanted to work with the West as long as it suited his own personal objectives. He led as a chief with his family's future legacy foremost in his mind. This included ownership of a Nairobi Hotel and Mamba Park as well as speculative investments in the new Rose Growing boom at Lakeside Naivasha.

'Oginga' Odinga KPU was more of a socialist, taking money from China and inspiration from Julius Nyerere in Tanzania. Group identity was assured when they, as well as Kenneth Kaunda in Zambia, followed in Mao's sartorial taste with a high collar buttoned suit instead of the 'fusty' colonial dress of coat and tails.

I had already nailed my colours to the mast in Kenya and Zimbabwe before so I felt very comfortable in these surroundings until I noticed that diners were looking at me in a strange way that made me feel nervous. Michael and Lou-Lou had arrived and we ordered some soup but I still felt discomfited. "Why are they staring at me?" I asked Ros but it was Michael who answered.

"Just look at yourself," he said with a slight touch of truculence that he must have learnt from Luke, "Whatever made you wear that thing?"

Lou-Lou came to my defence straight away. "You look lovely, Mum," she said, "You must have gone to a great deal of trouble with your hair and that flamingo dress."

Ros was non-committal but just said, "Yes, you do look lovely, Elda, but just take a look around the room, and at us for that matter. What do you see?" I looked, and then it dawned on me. All I could see were blue denim jeans and shirts, some with the 'Nyerere' high collar and I the luxuriant Flamingo in the centre of it all. I was embarrassed but I had to laugh and Ros and Lou-Lou joined in but Michael scurried off to the counter for a coke. "Not exactly my first lesson as a revolutionary," I said, "But I'll take it to heart just the same. You'd better find me a 'Dukas' (store/shop) before I begin to look conspicuous and maybe a bit ridiculous."

Ros laughed, "We could always sell you in the slave market," she said.

Michael had come back and chimed in, "We might even get a good price," but Lou-Lou thought they had gone far enough.

"Mum's trying to make change, isn't she, so give her a break," she said and gave me a big hug. I must admit that I felt quite emotional because when a mum and dad say that they are just 'finding space', all too often it ends in divorce and that is anathema for most kids. Had I thought this through?

"Take me to a Dukas (shop) quick," I said to Ros, "I need a change of just about everything top and bottom."

I sensed that she was amused but with the kids there, she just said, "Blue is beautiful around here and maybe white as a contrast." This sounded like sensible women out on a shopping spree but I sensed that it was much more than that.

Michael said, "Don't go too close to the Red-Light District." and laughed.

Lou-Lou chided him saying, "Give her a chance, Mike. She wants a new look, that's all."

Well, it wasn't quite all I knew, and I was finding out that even the simplest of changes seemed to have complications. Still, I loved them both dearly and said, "Why don't you come along?"

The response was immediate. "Not on your life," they said in unison. However, this teenage spirit of unity did not last long as Lou-Lou became mischievous.

"Mike won't be able to find time now. You won't see him for dust since he met up with Jilly van Basten. She takes him down the 'draav-in' in her dad's shiny Buick (she used the Afrikaans dialect with a touch of contempt)."

It seemed that the university politics had taken a hold already but how could they avoid it, I thought. I had not done much to keep them safe and sound, in fact, quite the opposite with my involvement at the Lakeside, and I began to feel guilty about that as well as the 'other' things. They knew a bit about my prison during the recent war, as it was part of the romantic story of Mum and Dad, but that was in the past and more pressing matters were on their young minds now. For example, how far would Michael go with Miss van Basten?

Domestic matters aside, it took a few days to get my 'place' sorted and soon I was ready for visitors, well, only one special visitor. Now, I felt that I was ready. Maybe this journal is not the best place to confide or even confine one's emotions to. I hesitate to say it but Ros was so patient with me that I blossomed like a flower to her every touch as she guided me around the petals of love. This was lovemaking as I had dreamt of it even whilst locked in the arms of Luke or Gordon. It was, well it was just different, perhaps with more of an emotional connection than I had known before and Ros knew exactly how to engage it with these words. *"No, not there or there but here…Look right into me and enter my eyes and my soul shall be waiting for you."*

I left her a small ring on the bedside table as a gesture of love and thanks, and she gave me a violet to press into my diary. This had been a most amazing experience and I knew that I was changed forever. I hoped that this would be a gradual formative change rather than an extreme revolutionary one, because there were others to consider when love (or was it lust?) is given licence. It was evident that Ros had no such hang-ups and the very next day she stated that she had to attend an important KPU meeting and I would be most welcome. "Without your Flamingos," she said with a laugh, and so we set out on a short walk away from 122 to a mysterious and secretive venue. We were greeted at the door of a large house by one of the people I had seen at the 'Kaff'.

"It's so good to see you again," she said, "My name is Miriam and this is my husband, Rufus," gesticulating to a man nearby. "Please, come in and make yourselves at home, there are only a few of us here and we are not officially connected to any political party. You may know Kito and a few others but we think that is best to remain anonymous in case there is trouble later."

I suppose that all of this was much as I thought it would be reminding me of my earlier days in Kenya when I had been imprisoned for subversion. I always seem to be 'against' something, I wonder why. However, although I do know that resistance for change must necessarily be secretive, the next statement took me by surprise as Miriam continued. "We take it as read that whatever is said here is and must remain confidential. We know to our cost what extremes some people went to during our war of liberation and we don't want to see them being repeated, do we?" This sounded a little bit like a threat as, with these words she recalled the barbaric methods of the Mau Mau, some of whom were in the room I would guess.

Now Rufus stood up and addressed the meeting with a wave, not unlike Kenyatta himself. "As my dear wife has explained, it is best for us to remain informal and we can leave our dear leader, Oginga, to deal with the political and legal business." he said, There is little doubt that Mzee Jomo is feathering his own nest and that of the many Msungus (whites) who support him. He talks big about a dynamic economy but it benefits the rich and leaves the poor scraping for a living and murmurs of 'Ndio' (yes), Bwana greeted his words.

Now he moved on to the substance of his argument namely that the agri-industrial rose enterprises by the lake were doing untold harm to the local economy as well as to a sustainable future. This was all music to my ears and I wanted to shout 'Ndio' as well but Ros nudged me and said 'Shush' as the next item took me by surprise. "There are many companies involved," said Rufus, "but Astrakan is one of the worst and we propose to do something about it, maybe just a peaceful raid on their greenhouses."

My heart sank. Why did it have to be Astrakan with Luke at the heart of their operation? There followed handshakes and goodbyes and soon after that, we left the meeting. I wanted Ros to reassure me as we walked home but she just said, "Not now, walls have ears, you know." I smiled at this incongruous remark as we walked along the banks of the river but I was still worried.

Back home, I sensed that a gap had opened up between us but Ros reassured me. "I hadn't told you this before," she said, "but I can tell you now that Luke resigned from Astrakan more than a month ago. Something to do with city investments I was told and nothing to do with the lake but I have my own doubts about that. I think that he left them because of his love for you. He had to make a personal choice and he made one, but at least, you are in the clear from any suspicion of helping him and Astrakan."

I was so relieved. My loyalties had also been sadly split a moment ago, but once again, Ros demonstrated that one strong love can accommodate two, and I sensed that she wanted the three of us to be as close as we could be. That was a big ask but I knew she was right.

"Let's go to bed, darling," I said.

The next morning, I awoke at dawn to the unusual sounds of seagulls squawking loudly as they swarmed down Uhuru Street and over our building and I wondered what they were trying to tell me this time. I put my hand out to feel Ros but she was not there, so I made a cup of tea and took it to her room next-door but there was no sign of her. I went sleepily back to my room and then saw a note that she had left. I sat on the bed and opened it gingerly and I could sense her presence and perfume in the room as I did so. This is what it said:

Dear Elda,

I'm sorry that I had to leave early but I didn't want to disturb you as you looked so lovely. The thing is that I have been chosen to join the raid to the Asrakan greenhouses in order to disrupt their growing plans for next year. We should be in and out in a flash and there are not many security guards there. I hope I'll be back in time for tea.

With luv
Ros x

PS I nearly forgot. Please get in touch with Luke if I don't get back soon. I know that he has a lovely surprise for you and the children. All my love, R

I didn't like the sound of the last bit but if Ros wanted me to see him, that might not be a bad thing after all. Maybe we could both go when he got back. Anyway, after a few days, I went to see Miriam to ask if she had any news "I'm so sorry," she said, "Eight of us went but only six came back and we haven't heard from Tom Theuri or Ros since. I'll keep you posted." I felt utterly deflated as I walked back to 122 flopping down on the 'Ros' side of my bed and cried for hours. Michael and Lou-Lou had heard tittle tattle in the KAFF so they came to visit and comfort me but it was no use. I was truly heartbroken and fearing the worst. After a silent meeting for about an hour, Lou-Lou said that she was going to phone the police. Michael was worried that Ros had done something illegal and might not want to be found. I lay on the bed, prone to the world but just able to raise my finger and point at Lou-Lou. This resulted in a brief visit from two pleasant officers but all I can remember is that they kept saying, 'private land you know, private land' after some (but not all) details were given to them and then they left.

Nothing happened for a few weeks and I had managed to get myself up when I had a message to go to the police station itself. At a desk, I was shown a bag and a young officer asked, "Do you recognise this, madam?" I said that I did and that it was indeed Ros' favourite bag. He then showed me the ring that I had given to her such a short while ago and said, "I am so sorry, madam. This bag was found at the Mamba Wildlife Park just outside the town. That park is owned by Kenyatta himself as well as the van Basten company and it was closed at the weekend. The bag was found inside the enclosures for the giant nile crocodiles but no other trace was found. I am so sorry."

I remember very little after that but I'm told that Michael and Lou-Lou brought me home and called a doctor who prescribed sedatives. Apparently, I tried to take the whole bottle as my depression reached a critical suicidal stage. Michael and Lou-Lou took it in turns to take on a 24-hour watch but it was nearly two weeks before I came out of it and when I did, I saw my lovely daughter. "Hello, Mum," she said, "it's good to have you back." Soon after that, Michael arrived and we all had a big hug. I showed them the letter in which Ros had suggested that I should go and see Luke and they both agreed.

"Let's all go," said Michael, and the next day we drove to Haven Farm. Lou-Lou had finished her studies and would stay on but Michael said that he would have to leave as he still had work to do.

"Work on Jilly van Basten?" said Lou-Lou rather insensitively. I could see she was not far off the mark as he blushed and left the room.

Chapter Five
Rosie

They had arrived the next day after an early start with a drive of about 75 miles from Nairobi to Naivasha behind them. Luke was waiting eagerly on the veranda with a big smile on his face and waved as they approached. "Welcome, welcome," he said, "Come on in and have some tea. You must be tired after your journey." He hugged them all separately and then together and then he said, "Oh, here's Ondago with the tea and some honey muffins that I know you love."

Luke could be so thoughtful at times and Elda had often wondered why he could be so inconsistent but for now, she was just glad to be back with him and the family, and the farm and, yes of course, the muffins.

He now led them around the side of the building and said, "Look around. What do you see?"

The first one to respond was Michael. "It's the Rondavels," he said, "they seem to be new and they're set in a circle as in a Masai style village."

"That's right, Mike," Luke responded, "I got the idea from Bill Maxwell's place up in Aberdare. He's turned his farm into a holiday tourist attraction up near Mt Kipiriri but that's 20 miles from Naivasha so I've got local advantage."

He did not tell Elda that he had begun the Rondavel project soon after she had left to 'spend time' with Ros in Nairobi, and well before news came of her murder. He did not tell her that initially his plan was to have two Rondavels and both were to be chapels. As a semi-retired Catholic priest, he planned to officiate at one of them and dedicate the other simply as 'A Chapel to God' and he planned to make it available for all and any other faiths. He did not tell her that when the chapels were built, he moved into one of them almost permanently and, recalling his strict Jesuit training, he chose to wear just a simple robe and cowl. He also did not tell her that from that first day, he began a long conversation of humility and repentance with God but there was no answer. Then, as if Elda was there herself, he awoke one morning to the screeches of her dawn birds, gulls, terns, flamingos and even the B52 pelicans, all doing their best to spur him to action. It might have been a dream, he had thought, but when he stepped inside, he heard the word of God and it said, "Elda is you and you are Elda, you have failed but now you must be there for her, should a misfortune occur."

It was months later when he heard of the news of the tragedy that took place but now he had finally been given a sense of priorities by the word of God. It was up to him now to build a new kind of future, and that is exactly what he had been doing over the last months.

***

Elda smiled at her husband. He could certainly get things moving when he wanted to and she noticed that there were eight Rondavels in two large circles. "What are the two circles for?" she asked.

Now he smiled at her. "I'm glad you noticed that, dear. It's a fact that the traditional Rondavel circular shape with the conical roof is a big draw for the tourists who like to 'go native'. I am now a member of the local Naivasha Tourist board and I've had considerable success with tours from Europe and elsewhere, but the others have been adapted to accommodate different functions. This one here," he said, pointing at the nearest, "is the regional HQ of the KWS, the Kenya Wildlife Society and the next one is a chapel. A non-denominational one, I hasten to add. The next are the offices of another private venture, namely the Haven Stud Farm that I set up last year with the OBTS, the Owners, Breeders and Trainers Society. I have a small staff and I can call on veterinary services from them when I need to. The main buildings of the NRJC, the Ngong Races Jockey Cub, are at the back. All of these ventures bring me some income and I hope you'll find this last one interesting."

His little family huddled around him waiting for this final revelation, but they had to wait until he led them to the back of the last Rondavel and there was a large sign with *ROSELDA* printed clearly at the entrance. With tears in his eyes, Luke pushed open the door and handed Elda a note in a perfumed envelope, which said:

Dear Elda,

Here is a present for you from your loving friend, Ros. Try to remember all the good times.

They all walked in slowly and as darkness turned to light, there before them was the most beautiful one-year-old yearling you might imagine, with ears pinned back in anticipation of something or other. Elda was amazed. "She's the most beautiful thing I've ever seen," she said, moving towards the horse and whispering, "Thank you, Ros, now you and I will be one for ever."

Roselda seemed to like the idea and arched her neck to nuzzle Elda's ample bosom for comfort.

Luke was silent for a long time, then said, "She'll need a lot of exercise and TLC for a few months but I'm sure she'll get it now."

At this point Lou-Lou butted in. "I reckon she wants a gallop right now. Can I take her? Can I? Please, Mum, can I?"

Elda turned to her daughter as she stroked the flowing mane and simply said, "Later, darling. We're just getting to know one another."

Meanwhile, Michael was getting bored. "Do you think there's any tea and muffins left, Dad?" he asked.

The next day broke with not a cloud in the sky as Elda sat and watched her dawn birds circling overhead. She viewed them with mixed emotions, hardly daring to trust that they signified good news this time but then the family arrived. Michael only stopped for a kiss on the cheek, saying he had to be off as soon as possible.

"Going to see silly Jilly, I suppose," said Lou-Lou, "make sure she doesn't have you for breakfast tomorrow."

Just at that moment, a slice of toast flew across the table and landed in Elda's lap and she retrieved it with a frown. "Can't even throw straight!" taunted Lou-Lou as Michael stormed off. Luke said nothing but to be honest, he was concerned that Michael had chosen a van Basten who was his main rival at the Lake.

With breakfast, over Lou-Lou could not wait to take Roselda through her paces. She had already been harnessed and was literally champing at the bit as was Lou-Lou. Elda was biting her nails as if she was watching Lou-Lou's first driving test in the family car, but this was different. Lou-Lou had charge of the most precious thing in her life so all she could say was, "Please, be careful, Ros." But what she had meant to say was, "Please, be careful, Lou-Lou, and come back safe."

Just then a van Basten truck pulled in to the yard and the driver got out. "Good morning, Jim," said Luke, "Just put the straw at the back. Thanks." He looked across at Elda and she was ashen faced. "What's up, darling?" he said, "All too much for you?"

She took his arm and said, "I know that face too. From Miriam's meetings before the Astrakan raid but do you see what I see?"

Luke looked hard as Jim was preparing to leave but just shrugged his shoulders and said, "I can't see anything out of the ordinary. I'd better sign his chit and he can go."

"When you do that," she said, "have a good look at his left ear, then come and tell me what you saw." Luke signed the chit and Jim drove away in a cloud of dust.

Now Luke looked intently at Elda. "He's wearing that diamond stud earing that Ros always wore, isn't he?"

She nodded with tears in her eyes as Luke took her hand gently. "I know some people in the police and in the courts and the judiciary, yes and Parliament," he said, "I'll get to the of bottom this, don't you worry." He meant what he said and this could be very difficult but then he remembered Daniel Kikonyo who was now Chief of Police in Nairobi. He had been a young police sergeant during the emergency when Luke had to give the last rites to condemn Mau Mau prisoners and had been revolted himself at their callous despatch on the gallows. He was on the platform that day when a woman called Fatuma asked for a blessing before she was hung. He had observed how Luke had shivered and cried so he had supported Luke's transfer to Eldoret that brought about Elda's wedding.

Many years had passed, but since Luke had built the chapel at Haven Farm, Daniel was a regular visitor with his wife and family and said he would like to help. This gave Luke the opportunity to give him the details of the Ros murder that had remained unknown up to now, namely the earing stud. A raid on Jim Kito's house revealed more details about Jim and his brother and their connection to van Basten.

Luke was content to let the case take its course after that so that Elda need not be involved. He knew that she had a forensic mind and would want to go over all the details of criminal proceedings as they developed, but he also knew that she was very emotionally vulnerable and he wished to protect her.

Roselda would be the key to her happiness and recovery so he developed a two-stage plan.

1/ Elda and Lou-Lou would remain at Haven Farm to train and prepare Roselda for the Ngong races which were about six months away.

2/ He would take Elda's old flat at No 122 Uhuru Street from whence he could make progress on the murder.

However, there was one problem that would have to be faced. Michael was still at the university in Nairobi and Luke knew that he would want to be involved. That was fine as far as it went but he also suspected that there would have to be a denouement with van Basten sooner or later and where would that leave Michael's burgeoning romance with Jilly? It might seem trite in the scheme of things, but he would have to walk on eggshells to avoid an impasse with his son so once again he apportioned tasks. "I'll be staying at 122 but I won't know anybody or where to look for clues so if you do all the important investigating work about who knows who, and I'll do the legal stuff when it comes to it. Will that be OK?' he asked.

Michael had nodded in agreement as he was behind with his coursework, not to mention that 1959 Paul Evans No 9 US hit was running through his head at the time.

Sittin' in the back seat, kissin' and a huggin' with Fred.

No eyes on the road but on the cinema silver screen at the 'draav-in' that Lou-Lou had dismissed so airily.

(Author's apologia for chronology but I couldn't resist it.)

***

Now we split the story into two.

1/ Elda continues her love affair with Roselda at the farm with Lou-Lou preparing for the Ngong races.

2/ Luke at 122 and the farm. There might have been a touch of déjà vu but he had actually never been there before, and that was one good reason to work with Michael who had a flat downstairs next to the KAFF.

1/ <u>Elda at the farm</u> "Gee Up Dobbin' was Elda's wake-up call each day as Roselda stretched her legs with a yawn. *How like Ros*, she thought, and then pushed the idea to the back of her mind. Roselda was to be the future and she and Lou-Lou did not have too much time to prepare her for racing. Luke had established a routine of sorts for two other mares stabled there but Roselda was a yearling and so the three of them had to start from scratch (Kenyatta carried a fly whisk but this was more a sign of Masai authority but Elda needed one for the flies). Luke had kitted out Roselda's stable very well with a 'medium' saddle that might have to be adjusted if Lou-Lou was to become an exercise rider, commonly known as a galloper before she could race. It was Elda's job to establish a rigorous training schedule but she had just the right kindness and patience to do so and the next three months were taken up in just that. She had designed a rosette for Roselda with the word *ROSIE* clearly shown. She thought it a bit odd to advertise the very product that she was opposing at the Lakeside but Roselda was unique and she loved her. It appeared that Rosie felt the same as she whinnied on seeing Elda or Lou-Lou approaching. As the day of the race meeting approached, Elda took advice about a jockey for the latest 'Kenya Derby', surely too much for Lou-Lou at this early stage. She was introduced to 'Tootsie Tambo' who had won just about everything in the past, but to be on the safe side, she ensured that Lou-Lou had all her riding proficiencies up to date and Tambo was given a provisional retainer until the nearer date. Meanwhile, she took up position three times a day at the gallops with stopwatch in hand to check on Rosie's

161

progress. She had designed a large placard that she could wave as Rosie went by and this gave the times of her most recent gallops. Elda also shouted the last one. "333," she called out loudly then 332 then 334 to finish the gallops on that particular day. There were now only four weeks to the meeting and Elda shook her head as a flush-faced Lou-Lou rode in.

"Sorry, darling," she said, "We're still not good enough, but as they say, you can lead a horse to water but you can't make her race." She smiled at her own phrasing but decided to have a long conversation with Roselda that evening. "Do it for me," she was going to say, "and if not for me, do it for Lou-Lou, she has worked so hard. And if not for us, do it for Ros, please do it for Ros." But how could she tell if Rosie understood?

The next day, she was out there again with placard and stopwatch in hand, and the timing went down and down. 332...330...325...320. It was the best they had ever done so all back to the stables for a lump of sugar. Who says that horses can't understand English?

This routine would have to go on for a few more weeks so there wasn't much time to catch up with Luke and Michael, but when they did, they were in for a shock.

2/ Luke at the farm Actually Luke came alone saying that Michael had work to do (as Lou-Lou grimaced) but he said it was best for him to come on his own this time because of the news that he brought. Michael had discovered that the 'driver' Jim Kito had a brother who worked at the Mamba Park and that he was on duty during that weekend. It would have been easy then to transport the body and for 'Stephen' with the key to leave the body in the Giant Nile Croc enclosure. Jim had meanwhile taken a fancy to the stud earring and perhaps Stephen had some pickings of his own. Now Luke came to the difficult bit. "They both work for van Basten," he said, "but proving his complicity in any way will be tough without confessions from the Kitos on promise of light sentences for aiding and abetting a crime. In that case, they would point fingers at their employer, and I'm advised that, even though guilt might not be proven, it is likely that extreme damages will be awarded. Paradoxically, we might gain as well.

Joint owner of the Mamba Park is Kenyatta and it is very likely that he will stand back as he might benefit himself from a van Basten bankruptcy but how can we break this to Michael? Lou-Lou and Elda looked at each other and smiled. "Didn't you know? That was over long ago," said Lou.

"Well, he might have told me to stop all my worrying." Luke complained, and then the three of them broke into laughter as they got up and hugged.

"I can't just leave it there," said Luke, "because I have to tell you that information has come to me that Tambo was one of the Astracan gang and he's under arrest as well. So what plans do you have for race day, Lou-Lou, my darling? I'm going to book tickets for Mum and me in the paddock as we are officially owners and trainers as well as breeders, so you'd better make it worth our while."

He was joking of course but Elda explained it rather better. "We are so proud of you that it doesn't matter where you finish," she paused and said, "just make sure you don't fall off and hurt my darling Rosie."

***

163

It was finally Derby Day at the Ngong races with top hats and parasols everywhere. Lou-Lou rode Roselda to a creditable 4th in the 'Yearling' handicap. Michael introduced a new girlfriend and Luke and Elda kissed as if it was their very first time, and it was in a way.

Ros had given them a chance and they had taken it, leaving St Elda and the dawn birds well behind them. They were now 'one' and that was just as it should be.

FIN

The Birds Take Flight

Foreword

It is a dark, damp and dreary morning on the shores of Lake Naivasha and even the dawn birds are not awake as a solitary figure stands alone and braced against the biting wind. This is Elda Bird (née Whitby and she is listening for the sound of hooves and the sight of a singular rider and horse to appear out of the mist. Then she sees them approaching the first hurdle rather faster than she would like.

Then, up, and away and over safely and she could afford a sigh of relief. These were extremely risky moments and much depended on attention to every detail and at present, it was going very well.

Her daughter Lou-Lou and her mount Roselda were looking good for the forthcoming 'Uhuru Cup' races at the Ngong races at Nairobi. These practice runs at the 'gallops' near Haven Farm by Lake Naivasha had preceded a decision to move race preparation closer to Nairobi where Lou-Lou and Roselda would find a new home at 'Lou-Lou's Livery Stable' in the old grounds of British Army HQ at Gil Gil. Here there was room for the stables as well as acres of room for a golf course and a prestigious Health and Leisure Spa Hotel.

This story will relate the events before and after the race as love and leisure, as well as sport and spite, are inextricable mixed up with local and international politics. To cut a long story short (which we won't), the race concludes with a spectacular crash with Lou-Lou *'flying'* headlong across the track after challenging for the lead, the favourite, the President's horse Lord Daladare was unmounted and Roselda was mortally wounded in the incident and had to be 'put down' at the trackside, and horrific scene to say the least.

Conspiracy theories were widespread and inspector Aziz had no suspects at first and then too many. If this wasn't bad enough, Lou-Lou, as well as Elda and Luke, all to take *flight* from the authorities before they could reach sanctuary in Aberdare. Another suspect was Tania who took a hurried *flight* somewhat further afield.

Chapter One
Lou-Lou's Livery Stable

The idea of a new and alternative centre of operations at Haven Farm in Naivasha had come to Elda and Luke after the murder of their friend Ros followed by their marriage a few years back.

The issue then as now had been over the use of the Lake's finite resources for ecological, sustainable fisheries or commercial rose growing for the international market with ruthless speculators bent on expansion. Suspecting that she might be a target, Ros had presented them with a lovely yearling, Roselda, and they had begun to create a new equestrian centre with the slogan *HORSE BEFORE THE CART*, which they now began to transfer in part to Gil Gil with further plans to expand into leisure activities. In this way they hoped to make a case for more sustainable and environmental developments, locally as well as in the whole of Kenya itself.

A few more practice runs and then Lou-Lou travelled the 100 miles, 'horse box and all' to Nairobi and arrived full of ideas and enthusiasm.

On her first visit, she was somewhat taken aback by the remaining vestiges of the British Army and the King's

African Rifles that remained scattered around an old Land Rover here and a dilapidated jeep there greeted her as she stepped inside the barred gates and wire fencing and she was pleased to note that there was no guard on show...yet! The British had evacuated some time ago and Gil Gil was just another property ripe for development and Elda and Luke had picked it up rather cheaply without too many questions asked.

Lou-Lou now approached an imposing-looking building with ragged Union Jacks still fluttering and a massive and imposing oak door with a sign that said, *BRITISH HQ, NO ENTRY*, and Lou-Lou looked around rather nervously before she entered. She was immediately in a large panelled room with signs for *2nd Regiment* or *Medical Centre* on display. In the dim light, she could make out an imposing staircase with portraits of British Generals and military victories on show at every step. Then, as she mounted carefully, she was somewhat surprised to see another person; in fact, a sentry on-guard. Up to now she had been alone but her relief was soon expunged by rather blunt army statement, "No entry," the sentry said, with a somewhat threatening tone "unless you have an appointment in writing and in triplicate."

Lou-Lou felt sorry for him as she had visions of the not-so-scary Lion in the *Wizard of Oz*. He was a young British corporal with an accent from Liverpool, and she supposed that he wished he was back at home by the banks of the Mersey.

Why he was still there was a mystery to her, and probably to him as well. Thinking fast, she produced a jumble of official papers with a waft of her hand before proceeding up the stairs and bypassing him with a very sweet, "Thank you, corporal, you are so kind. I'll see myself up."

At the top, there was another massive oak door, which she pushed open gently. She half expected to see a dozen or so clerks destroying any incriminating evidence that the Army did not want to leave behind but there were none. Then a man appeared from under a desk and smiled politely.

"Miss Bird, I presume," he said, "Captain Tom Bentley at your service, I have been expecting you and I'll soon be done, then you'll have the place all to yourself. I'm just sorting out the last of the 'Crown Jewels' as we liked to call them but really they are mostly about kitchen provisions rather than army manoeuvres. Still, you never know. We did find an item screwed up in the bin last week with the heading *TOP SECRET* but it was in code and I had to send it away to be translated. I don't suppose I'll ever know what it was about. Anyway, I've got a transfer to a new base in Aberdare now so if you're ever up that way, please pop in and see me. Meanwhile, good luck with Dobbin," he said with a smile, and then he was gone and Lou-Lou felt strangely alone.

She moved carefully across the dusty floor and sat down in the one-office chair that did not seem to be broken. In front of her were a pile of paper on a very traditional roll top desk with drawers that seemed to be empty. However, she did note that one of them was still locked and she wondered what was in it. At the back of the room were two very comfy settees and a large safe that also seemed to be locked. *Curiosity killed the cat,* she thought, *and this won't do; I've got to get out in the yard to get organised but maybe I'll pop back later for a snooze.* She laughed at herself but it was nice to feel that she was her own boss for a while at least. Down the stairs and out into the yard and this is what she had come for. A dusty parade ground about the size of a football pitch with stables on one side and various lock-ups on the others, gave her an immediate incentive to go and fetch Roselda to bring her 'home'. She had been temporarily left overnight at another stables and Lou-Lou already missed her. It was a long walk but well worth it as Roselda whinnied her welcome.

These stables were more of a commercial setup with more than 20 horses, stabled with grooms, caring for their every need. Lou-Lou spoke to the person in charge, who was 'Madame' Toqueville, with a whole host of racing victories behind her in Kenya and in Europe, even the Arc de Triomphe on one occasion. Madame introduced herself as 'Babette' (Babs for short) and soon she and Lou-Lou were getting-on like a house on fire. "You must come to visit again," said Babette, "when you are settled, of course. What's more, I have a waiting list for stabling and I could recommend two or three geldings to you, if you like, just until you become viable. Also, I have a few trainee stable girls and young men who might benefit from a change. No guarantees, mind you. Two of them are on probation for theft but I tend to believe in second chances, don't you? By the way, that's the name of one of my entries for the big race so I hope she won't fall with Roselda."

She laughed, a lovely tinkling musical laugh, and Lou-Lou found herself hesitating for a moment or two before replying, "Perhaps they might share a gallop one day, first let me get her home and settled in and we can chat about it tomorrow."

"Please send your stable hands over in the morning so that I can check them out and so that I can get started in the yard, if they are suitable. Also please ask any owners to get in touch about stabling, if you don't mind. Thank you so much. I hope we might share a sundowner soon, so bye for now."

It was that easy. With Bab's help, Rufus Tambo, a young Kikuyu, was soon clearing the yard and Helga Noorkop, a tall Swedish girl whose father was the Swedish 'charged' affairs, had begun to welcome Roselda's stablemates when they arrived. First was 'She Loves You', a dappled grey owned by Paul and Stella Royce, followed by two or three more geldings over the next few weeks.

Helga was a godsend, a natural 'horse whisperer', and a love affair soon blossomed in stable number two. Babs organised a welcome party and soon Lou-Lou began to feel more at home. She now had a few more helpers in the yard but squabbles sometimes arose, especially between the different Kenyan tribes. Tambo was a Kikuyu but two others, who had been recommended were Ondago who was a Lou, and Solomon who was a Somali, with no love lost between any of them.

Fortunately, Helga introduced her two sisters so there was a happy harmony in their stalls.

Chapter Two
Love, Leisure and Larceny

Lou-Lou knew that the new stables would not be welcomed by everyone but she was surprised to see a cavalcade of police and army vehicles pull up at the stables a few days later at 6 am. The army led the way with rifles at the ready as the main building seemed to yield very little and the soldiers soon re-appeared emptyhanded and shaking their heads before driving away. It was then that she was approached by the senior police officer in uniform but with very relaxed manner.

"I'm sorry about all this, Miss Bird," he said, "perhaps we should have warned you, but we were rather hoping to catch someone removing some documents. You see, we had received a tipoff but obviously it was too late. By the way, I understand that Rufus Tambo is working here, an 'informant' you might say and I have found that he is a good source of information from time to time. The safe was virtually empty when I got there but there were a few papers left behind, one of which was headed:

HIM GOV TOP SECRET Attached is MI5 intelligence report on suspected on suspected Russian/Kenyan proposals for development of Atomic-Hydro Electric facilities on Lake Victoria under guise of 'ecological research'

Unfortunately, there were no further details but I immediately realized the importance of the document, given the imminent nuclear talks involving all international rivals including the Russians, British and Americans in Adis Adaba.

However, I was cautious not to reveal my find until I had made further enquiries; for example, if Ondago did steal the document, who might have paid him for the information and who might be the eventual buyer? I needed all this to make a case so I asked Rufus to track him down and I'm still waiting but it could take some time."

He paused and continued mischievously, "Waiting for you maybe, but I could always come and 'muck out', if you'd like me to."

He laughed again and Lou smiled as well. "I hardly know you," she said, "and we wouldn't want to muddy your pristine spotless uniform, would we?" Suddenly she flushed again and chided herself for being such a pushover.

"Let's be serious," she said eventually, "please tell me, how I can help you as I have other work to do and another appointment."

The officer now bowed gracefully. "Inspector Aziz Shah at your service, ma'am," he said, "Some say that I'm a distant cousin of the Aga Khan but maybe I might impress you another way. Well, at least I can try," he added and with this parting shot, he waved and drove away. Lou-Lou wondered what the heck was going on. Three potential lovers all in one day was just too much so she hurried upstairs to find solace in one of the old but very comfortable settees in the ward room.

Lou-Lou was now 22 and no stranger to love affairs but she always claimed that they were 'nothing serious'. Now she lay down on the comfy cushions and opened her journal turning to the pages marked *Personal*. This is what she had written:

NEW YEAR'S DAY PARTY

I met Colin van Osten and liked him at once. He was adventurous out on the Veldt and in bed but then I found out that he was an 'Afrikaans Ranger', I should have known from the name of course but he was such a dish.

MAY DAY

Introduced to Sir Stephen Mackenzie at the Taylor's. A touch of the 'Happy Valley' about him attracted me but when he invited me to a 'house party' in Mombasa I got scared thinking of the slave trafficking that went on there, so I refused and he didn't ask again.

1 JULY

Old friend Tom Sharpe turns up and suggests the usual but my plate had gone cold.

1 AUGUST

Personals and dating on hold, I take Roselda to Nairobi with 'offers' in my pocket.

Now she closed the book and was soon asleep as Aziz appeared in a silken bejewelled robe whilst Babs performed a dance with five veils and Tom sulked in the corner. She herself was only covered by a cotton sheet as Aziz approached and she held out her arms. Then there was an almighty crash as she knocked over a small table and awoke with start.

"Damn and damn again," she said, "just as it was starting to get interesting."

Despite this diversion, work at the stables continued apace with the landscaping of the golf course as well as the foundations of a grand hotel to rival others in the area and it was pretty obvious to Lou-Lou that she needed help at a management and organizational level as well as in the yard. To this end, she persuaded her brother Michael to join her as MD projects to supervise these new ventures. In addition, as staff came and went, she decided to hire an MD for 'Recruitment and staff Relations', and after some interviews and clearance with the police, courtesy of Aziz who had some contacts at the Russian embassy, she settled on a Russian *émigré* called Tania. It goes without saying that Lou-Lou was not aware that Aziz and Tania were already clandestine lovers and Tania had made it clear the she would brook no rivals either. "It's me or nobody," she had said, "I've seen the way you look at Lou-Lou but there'll be no extras to your harem in that direction; and keep your eyes off of Helga's sisters as well."

Tania was indeed grateful for the job and had let Aziz know it in the way that she knew best; between the sheets and sometimes in the hay.

They had both agreed that this would have to be a most discrete affair so meetings were usually after dark in selective and seedy venues including stables in the straw amongst the small of leather and the odd objection from a resident horse.

Of course, Tania still had her duties at the stables with Lou-Lou and Michael as they prepared for race day. This meant work of different kinds in marketing and admin to take some of the burden off Lou-Lou's shoulders but at least Lou-

Lou might find a bit of time to relax a little in her own quarters that she had prepared to her taste with a large four-poster and shower unit, not to mention subtle lighting, cushions and coverlets to die for.

One day as dusk approached, she found herself alone in the building and stripped bare as she approached the inviting shower. It gurgled in a musical fashion and she recalled the sound of Babs' tinkling tones as she now slipped beneath the cotton covers and fell fast asleep. *Maybe I'll have another erotic dream*, she thought as she drifted off. So it was that the night passed peacefully until dawn when she began to relive a dream that she'd had before very recently with Aziz and others in the cast. She remembered it well and, as in the dream, she held out her arms to her dreamy lover. She shut her eyes firmly but then she opened them, and there he was; no dream but a real firm muscular Aziz touching her gently.

"My darling, *Ma Cherie*," he said, and she wondered what other languages he might use in this situation; English, French or even Arabic.

He was not going to get away with it this time, she decided as she flung aside her covers and said, "Do you like what you see, Aziz? Now kiss me, touch me and give me your hand, yes…there." It is probably best to draw a curtain over the next few hours but when Lou-Lou awoke Aziz was gone. She put her hand out in a hopeful gesture but could only find a little note. '*Ma Cherie,*' it said, '*Merci Lou-Lou, I hope that we might find time for another rendezvous quite soon. A bientot, Aziz.*'

She screwed the note up and threw it across the room but after all, what had she really expected?

Maybe it was all a dream, she thought, but as she looked across the room, she saw a crumpled piece of paper just about to be blown away by the breeze. She hurried to get up, but then sank back again with a sigh as it wafted out of the door.

There must have been something in the air as springtime came and went and the race date became even closer. A certain heightened activity was evident in all sections of the enterprise and it was inevitable that Lou-Lou and Michael and Tania would be drawn closer together as plans were made. Lou-Lou spent some of her time with Babs, gleaning all the advice that she could from this experienced horse-lover. Babs explained that all success with horses depended on a mutual love between owner, rider, stable girl and horse. "It's the same with everything," she explained, "Love makes the world go around, *n'estce pas*?" She smiled and laughed that 'tinkly' laugh that had attracted Lou-Lou in the first place.

It was still there, that feeling of warmth as before, but Aziz had decided to be more careful with her emotions. "Let's take a stroll," she suggested, offering her hand to Babs, "Let's just go and see how your new foals are doing." In this way a loving friendship was secured, and thoughts of any romantic love were pushed into the long grass for the time being.

This was not the case with Michael and Tania as their paths continued to cross on a daily basis.

One might say that she had almost become his deputy as he attended meetings at the Nairobi Chamber of Commerce and met with other important political and influential businessmen men and women. Actually he was not that proactive in the detailed work himself preferring the social side of things. "Ask Tania," he would say if a decision was called for but there was method in his 'madness'. On any pretext, he could call Tania to his office, just off the main reception area, and, after a suitable amount of business chat, he might easily persuade her to sit on one of those settees for preliminaries before advancing to his inner sanctum. He was serious about his courtship but to her, he was a bit of a diversion from her main aim, who was Inspector Aziz, as have just seen.

She just adored his mystery as well as his melodious voice, his smart uniform and the excitement and romantic appeal of her own 'Sheikh of Arab'; but Michael would do for now.

His office was bedecked with flags and illustrations of Gordon's disastrous camping up the Nile to Khartoum, and these provided the backdrop to an adventure of a different kinds as Michael took Tania in his arms. Gordon would not be rescued by them today…that's for sure, as Michael wallowed in a kind of seventh heaven under imaginary desert skies, Unfortunately, he somewhat put off his stroke when the phone rang for a message but Tania ignored it with a smile. "Come on, General," she said, "let me get you before the Mahdi does!" Another half hour of stroke and counter stroke eventually brought action to a halt; one must admit with a sense of anti-climax rather than the opposite.

The siege was over as Tania retreated to the bathroom and viewed her message. It was from Aziz *Come soon, ma Cherie* it read and she was quite excited until she remembered that she had picked up a scrap of paper from the yard earlier that day. It had been addressed to *Ma Cherie, Lou* and Tania immediately knew that she had a rival, and that her rival was none other than her boss, Lou-Lou Bird and she didn't 'do' rivalries. *Something would have to be done*, she thought, *but what?*

Chapter Three
Race Day

Such romantic diversions were all very well but each week had brought race day closer and closer until finally the day arrived when Lou-Lou and Roselda would be tested against an international field at Ngong including the President's horse, Lord Deladare. This name was a somewhat 'political' play on words, following the contribution of Lord Delamere to Kenyan society, and maybe pointing to Kenyatta's favour for a 'status quo ante', and against reform movements such as that of Elda and Luke at Haven Farm now with their own 'Trojan Horse', name of Roselda at the races.

Kenyatta would be in the Presidential Box as expected alongside the 'most favoured guest', the Sheikh of Abu Dhabi, with his own posse of pedigree horses in the race. Next to him would be the Russian Ambassador on his left and the British Equerry next along the line, notably a minor position as Kenyatta sorted out his international priorities. The US Ambassador had refused as invitation and this, in itself, rather demonstrated the antipathy of the US to Kenyatta's KANU party at this time, given the US hostility to Russia. So it was a balancing act for the President, trying to keep all potential allies sweet and, one foot wrong, a scandal or an avoidable accident might easily upset the applecart one way or the other.

The same was somewhat true of his domestic policies as he attempted to balance the economic future of his country with the many calls for environmental and other protections as called for by Luke and Elda and many others. Elda still placed her faith in the dawn birds over Naivasha, a superstition you might say, but one that she took extremely seriously. Luke understood and supported her, although he didn't agree. "It's an article of faith with her," he would say, "A bit like Bread and Wine for us Catholics." So on this prestigious day of the Nairobi races, she sat on the veranda at Haven Farm and looked skyward for a sign of her birds but at 6 am it was still a little early for them. She waited patiently and then, yes there they were, far in the distance but heading south just as she planned to do herself.

"Hello, my lovelies," she called out over the miles, "Please look after Lou-Lou and Roselda on this special day. I'll see you at the races a bit later on." With that, she was tempted to cross herself in solidarity with Luke but he was getting the car ready, but she did it just the same 'to make sure'. Then as she turned to climb into the passenger seat, she took a last look upward and wished that she hadn't. The birds were advancing all right but they were screeching and squabbling instead of circulating in polite circles as they usually did and her face fell as she felt a sense of imminent disaster before Luke drove away.

"Is everything OK, darling?" he asked encouragingly.

"Yes, fine," she replied, "Let's get going before the crowds waving support for riders and horses reach as they parade before the race begins."

Elda pressed Luke's hand and just said, "I love you Luke," as they viewed the spectacle. First in line was the favourite, the president's horse Lord Deladare ridden by the champion jockey, Jack Standish Next was Lady Dare, Deladare's stablemate with Anne Flynn from Ireland on board. Then came Brittania and Marvel, followed by Roselda and the others proceeding in line to the starting area, where they all circled around looking for an advantageous place before the race began.

Then they heard the sound that they and the vast crowd had been waiting for. *THEY'RE OFF!* was the signal for the race to start and the loudspeakers carried the race commentary as it proceeded…

'Ladies and gentlemen, hold on to your hats as this looks like being a very close race as they now approach fence number one. Here they come and it seems that Marvel is in the lead followed closely by Lady Dare, but at fence two, Roselda has crept up to third with Lord Deladare not far behind and outsiders Spartan and She loves you ridden by teenager Ruth Royce up there as well. (Here the commentary crackled and got lost entirely for a few moments until the horses approached the last in a close bunch)…

Bzzzcracklle…*bzz…Now it's' jockey Ujukwu who leads but no…his mount Rift Valley has baulked at the last fence and impeded the field…I can't see what's going on! It's a real melee but it looks like Roselda is down after colliding with Lord Deladare. Both jockeys have flown through the air as their mounts collapsed under them, Oh the tragedy! But no, I see that Standish is on his feet but Lou-Lou Bird lies prone as the back markers try to avoid her. Meanwhile, Deladare is limping away but Roselda is in a heap with back legs twitching and it doesn't look good at all as Lou-Lou Bird crawls towards the stricken animal in an attempt to save her but it seems in vain. Now the paramedics have picked her up and placed her in the ambulance, despite her protests as it speeds away to the hospital with lights flashing and sirens blazing, it looks very bad...Stay with me, stay with me, it's a grisly scene but I must look up the track to the finishing line and tell you about the result as the rest of field cruise across the line. Yes, it looks like Rift Valley is the winner with Abu Abu, one of the Sheikh's horses, second and that will please our honoured guest, won't it? Looking back now, I see a group of white coated vets around Roselda and I fear the worst but I'll try to get an interview with the winner as soon as I can but wait! The result has been challenged and now we have a statement from the race stewards as follows:*

The unfortunate incident at the Ngong races today calls for an inquiry. The Stewards assert that jockeys Ujukwu and Bird had both acted dangerously and 'with intent', so the race has been awarded to Abu Abu until the matter could be resolved. Jockeys and owners are to be arrested and questioned as soon as possible.

***

Up in the grandstands, Elda and Luke listened with dismay to this announcement. They did not trust the 'authorities' one way or the other but fortunately they already had a plan, should things go 'wrong'. Of course, they had not expected such a drama, but they had friends in Aberdare who could be relied on, and they knew that Lou-Lou must be spirited away before she and they had to face accusations likely to be hostile. The President could not be seen to show weakness, especially with the Adis Abiba talks on the horizon. He would be looking for scapegoats and they were determined that Lou-Lou would not be one of them.

So, at midnight, with guards drowsy and a little bit drunk, a private black hearse drew up in a backstreet by the hospital. Two gowned and top-hatted figures moved rapidly to collect a 'funeral' package and place it in the back before moving off to head north with a silent whisper. It was a long journey past Naivasha to the Aberdare Hospital where Lou-Lou was finally taken inside, sedated and made comfortable for the night. Elda and Luke had followed and now breathed a sigh of relief.

Chapter Four
Now You See Her...

Meanwhile, and far away from Aberdare, Aziz had other problems on his mind, namely the theft of the Gil Gil documents but he had not entirely forgotten about Lou-Lou and their brief 'affair'. He therefore sent a warm note for her recovery to the Gil Gil address @Lou-Lou's Livery stables because he did not know where she had gone after the race. However, his investigations in Nairobi were proving fruitful and with the aid of Tambo, he had tracked down Ondago who freely admitted to the theft and stressed that it was a political act on behalf of the KPU, the rival party to KANU. To show good faith, he said that he would take Aziz to their cave stronghold at the Karukura Falls and introduce him to their leader, leaving Aziz to negotiate a 'deal' for the Gil Gil documents.

The next day dawned, dark and blustery, as Ondago and Aziz set out for the caves, and their journey got even more dramatic as they approached the falls along a slippery slope with gulls and terns hounding them at every step. At the cave entrance, they were greeted by a group of armed Lou warriors primed for action with shields, spears, pangas and rifles, just to make sure. Their leader stepped forward dramatically.

"*Me ShakaLuo*," he said, 'Speak!" Aziz looked up at this huge and imposing figure, *all of seven foot*, he thought, and with a name Shaka redolent of the famous Zulu chief himself. "Speak!" He repeated.

Aziz turned helplessly to Ondago. "What shall I say?" he muttered.

"Offer them Pombe Booze," replied Ondago.

"But I don't have any," replied a hapless Aziz, "Wont money do?"

Ondago laughed. "Look at them," he said, "half-starved and drugged most probably. Offer them Tusker and we can get some from the Dukas down the hill."

Aziz did not want to argue and began to slide down the muddy hill, followed by a group of warriors who prodded him with their assegais until he arrived at a little shop that seemed to sell everything. A sign pointed to a door marked *JAMBO* (Hello) and Ondago went inside, coming out soon after with about 50 bottles of Tusker lager. He handed it over to Shaka in exchange for a simple envelope and then the chattering mob left the two of them along outside the shop. Aziz felt strangely cheated as he opened it rather gingerly. He had expected a bulky package of papers but this is what he read:

Gil Gil documents ref GG2214 retrieved from British Army HQ now acquired by KPU to be sold at auction at Room 333 on Sunday, 2 July, at midnight at the Norfolk Hotel River Street Nairobi KPU will carry all relevant documents to the sale

Aziz looked at Ondago as if he could kill him but Ondago just said, "Take it easy, Bwana, you have got what you wanted, haven't you? We'll go to the auction and you can see for yourself who buys them. As a matter of fact, I can assure you that there will be only one bidder, so we must make ourselves scarce if we are to see who it is."

Room 333 at the Norfolk was actually a small cinema/theatre with a curtained stage, exit left and exit right, with red velvet semi-circular seats of 12 in rows of 12. Ondago and Aziz had arrived early and sat down quietly in the back row and waited under an Exit light that had been broken.

After about 20 minutes, Shaka appeared from under the exit left sign with six men, walked to a group of seats close by and sat down. Further ten minutes passed before a second group of five appeared from stage right and sat down in a group facing the others. Conspicuously, however, the central seat in their front row was left blank until a hooded figure appeared from the back of the stage and sat down. Aziz sensed that it was a woman as she held out her hand, palm upward as if to seek a gift or present. Shake responded immediately and moved forward to place a large bulky bundle in her hand. She passed it to her left and signalled the man on her left to pass an envelope to him. No words were exchanged as both groups turned to leave. As Aziz craned forward to see, his prayers were answered as the woman turned to her 'imaginary' audience with a bow as she stood momentarily under the exit right beam that lit up her face. It was Tania! He looked again but she was gone, and he suddenly felt weak at the knees and sat down.

"You OK, Bwana?" said Ondago, "You see what you wanted?"

Aziz was confused as he looked at Ondago. "Yes," he said, "but then again…No."

Now it was Ondago's turn to be confused so he waited and just said, "We go now, Bwana. Business done," and they left.

By the time he got home, Aziz thought that he had rationalised the whole situation. Of course, he knew that Tania was Russian and he supposed it was not really surprising to find that she was a Russian agent. Yes, the plans were for Kenyan and Russian collaboration at Lake Victoria, but up to now they had thought that this was a secret between them. Now Tania's intervention meant that all preparation could be covered up and halted, making any accusations by the Allies of Russian nuclear interference in Africa at Adis Abiba ultimately deniable. There were shades of the Cuban missile crisis here as a ready response to any questions would be, *"What plans? What preparations? Please send your U2s and you'll see that we have nothing to hide."*

Now Aziz was faced with a dilemma and decided that the best way for him to proceed would be to notify the President that he could 'call off the hounds' with regard to any political conspiracy at the race track thus clearing Lou-Lou, but first, he decided to meet Tania at a secret location to clear the air after the race. After all, she had not known that he was at the 'hand over' but he just said that he was 'desperate' to see her. She responded positively and they met for dinner 'and afters' at the Hotel Belvedere. Things were much the same as before but, although Aziz probably overdid his favourite line of *"jet'aime"*, Tania was still swept along in the passion of the many moments until dawn as he got up to leave.

"Important court case," he said, "All that stuff about the accident. I'll phone you tonight."

"Surely time for another little kiss," she said, "after all I've done for you. Accident, you say. Well, let me tell you that it was no accident. So who do you think it was who paid Ujukwu to push Rift Valley across the track so that your precious little 'Madame Lou-Lou' would fall in a heap?" She laughed and reached out again mischievously, but Aziz had already stepped out of reach.

He just said, "Let's talk tonight," and with that he was gone, striding down the corridor with gritted teeth but also seething inside.

Now it was clear to him what he must do and that night, he led a raid on Tania's flat only to find that she too had 'taken flight'. Enquiries at the consulate and airport revealed that she had caught the 1030 Aeroflot flight to Moscow and Aziz didn't know whether to feel cheated or pleased that he did not have to confront her. He did find a note addressed to him at her flat that said, *Ma cher Aziz, au revoir jet'aime toujours, Tania.* In other times, he might have cherished it but this time he just threw it away in disgust.

Chapter Five
A Safe Landing

It was dawn on the banks of Lake Naivasha when Lou-Lou and her family got to hear of their 'reprieve' through this surprising Presidential Press Release following the debacle at the races:

*My dear friends, you will be pleased to hear that the perpetrators of the unfortunate incident at Ngong have been apprehended and punished and my dear wife and I thank you for love and support in these dangerous days. As we move on to a united future here in Kenya with KANU and the KPD working closely together, I am pleased to announce a new SDR on the banks and region of Lake Victoria. A **Sustainable Development Region** will be created giving room for experimental work as well as funding for existing projects. This venture will demonstrate our commitment to a progressive and peaceful future for All Kenyans.*

Luke was the first to comment. "He's a genius, that man," he said, "He's dealt with the past and the future in such a way that everyone supports him," he paused, "that is if anyone believes him."

There were smiles around the table with Elda looking thankfully to the heavens to share this moderate victory with her dawn birds. Lou-Lou held hands with her husband Tom (Did I mention that she had married Captain Tom Bentley and now there might be chicks on the way?)

Michael now rose from the table, held up his glass and said "Let's all raise our glasses to the birds and that includes them up there as well as us."